A KEY TO THE ADULT MALES OF THE BRITISH

CHIRONOMIDAE

(Diptera)

the non-biting midges

by

L. C. V. PINDER

Freshwater Biological Association

Illustrated by
ANGELA M. MATTHEWS

Vol. 1   The Key

FRESHWATER BIOLOGICAL ASSOCIATION
SCIENTIFIC PUBLICATION No. 37
1978

SBN 900386 32 0
ISSN 0367-1887

CONTENTS OF VOLUME ONE

INTRODUCTION

Despite their ubiquity, very little is known about the life cycles or ecology of individual species of Chironomidae — the non-biting midges. This is largely because of the difficulty of identifying the larvae, since very few have been adequately described. It is frequently necessary to rear larvae through to the adult stage for positive identification, and it is only in this way that the data necessary for the eventual compilation of a comprehensive key to larvae can be accumulated.

Previous keys to the adults of British chironomids by Edwards (1929) and Coe (1950) were based exclusively on dried material. Indeed, Coe stated that "In no circumstances should adult specimens be preserved in spirit or other liquid as . . . identification of the specimen may become practically impossible". This argument was effectively countered by Schlee (1966) and preservation in spirit is nowadays the usual practice. This new key is based upon characters which are readily observed in such material.

The two keys mentioned also suffer from several other drawbacks. In particular, they are insufficiently illustrated, and numerous additions and alterations to the British list have been made since their publication. Whereas Coe's key dealt with 389 species, a total of 448 are listed in the recently revised check-list of British insects (Kloet & Hincks 1975). Of this total, several are not included in the present key. Generally these omissions relate to specimens which have subsequently been shown to be misidentified, but a small number have been omitted because it has not been possible to examine specimens of British provenance. The total number of species included is 439.

NOMENCLATURE

One further factor which influenced the decision to produce this new key to adult males is the confusion over nomenclature with which the student of the Chironomidae is confronted. The main reason for the confusion is that two systems of nomenclature have evolved side by side. On the one hand F. W. Edwards who was primarily concerned with the morphology of the imagines preferred to use large, broadly defined genera, whereas Thienemann and others working mainly with the immature stages favoured a system which employed smaller, more closely defined genera. More recently a good deal of progress has been made towards reconciling the two systems through consideration of all stages. The result is that the nomenclature used by Edwards (1929) and Coe (1950) differs substantially from that which is generally accepted throughout Europe and increasingly in North America.

The nomenclature used in this key follows that of the recently revised *Check list of British insects* (Kloet & Hincks 1975) which takes account of the developments in taxonomy up to 1975. There are, however, a few differences. The main one is that I have followed Saether (1976) regarding the separation of the genus *Prodiamesa* and its allies as a distinct subfamily (Prodiamesinae). Table 1 (p. 18) shows the major subdivisions of the Chironomidae as recognized in this key.

Changes in generic nomenclature which have been published since the revised *Check list of British insects* have not been included. The most notable of such changes are due to Saether (1977) (viz: *Microcricotopus* Thien. & Harn. to *Nanocladius* Kieffer, *Paracladopelma* Lenz to *Cladopelma* Kieffer and *Leptochironomus* Pagast to *Microchironomus* Kieffer).

MORPHOLOGY

The main features of the adult male chironomid are shown in fig. 1. The most obvious difference between the sexes is that the female antennae are much less densely plumose.

The following simple key will serve to distinguish chironomid midges from other Diptera with which they might otherwise be confused.

1   Antennae usually long and slender, consisting of at least 6 visible segments—Suborder NEMATOCERA   **2**

—   Antennae with fewer than 6 visible segments—
                      Suborders BRACHYCERA & CYCLORRHAPHA

2   Costa extending around the entire margin of the wing—
            Families CECIDOMYIDAE, CULICIDAE, DIXIDAE, PSYCHODIDAE,
            PTYCHOPTERIDAE, THAUMALEIDAE, TIPULIDAE, TRICHOCERIDAE

—   Costa confined to the anterior wing margin—   **3**

3   Ocelli (simple eye spots) present, arranged in a triangle between the compound eyes—
            Families ANISOPODIDAE, BIBIONIDAE, MYCETOPHILIDAE, SCATOPSIDAE

—   Ocelli absent—   **4**

4   Antennae bare—   Family SIMULIIDAE

—   Antennae 'hairy'—   **5**

5   Vein M forked—   Family CERATOPOGONIDAE
—   Vein M simple (fig. 5)—   Family CHIRONOMIDAE

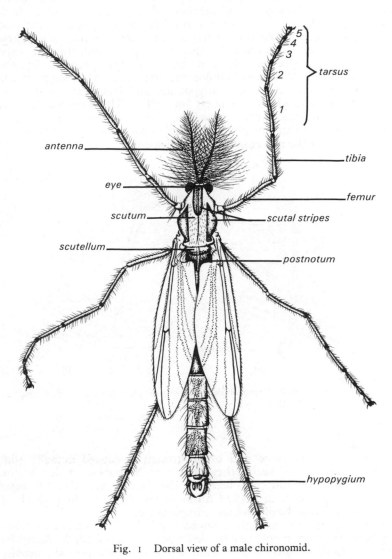

Fig. 1 Dorsal view of a male chironomid.

The *antenna* of the male (figs 2A & 2B) consists of a large globular second segment or *pedicel* and a *flagellum* of up to 14 segments, which normally carry whorls of long setae giving the antenna its characteristic plumose appearance.   The pedicel has usually been regarded as the first antennal segment or *scape*, but as Saether (1971) points out, the true scape is the usually suppressed segment basal to the pedicel.   In the Chironominae and the Orthocladiinae the last antennal segment is the longest (fig. 2A) whereas in the Tanypodinae and Podonominae it is the penultimate segment which is longest (fig. 2B).   The *antennal ratio* is often a useful taxonomic character, and this is here defined as the length of the longest flagellar segment plus any segment distal to it, divided by the combined length of the preceding flagellar segments.

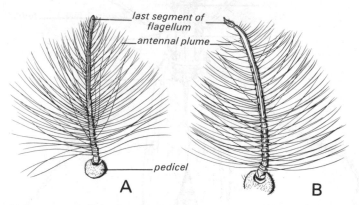

Fig. 2   Male antennae of: A, *Orthocladius thienemanni* (Orthocladiinae); B, *Procladius choreus* (Tanypodinae).

The *eyes* are very large and often strongly produced dorsally (fig. 3A).   In a number of species they appear to be pubescent due to the presence of fine microtrichia between the facets (fig. 3B).   *Frontal tubercles* (fig. 3A) occur in many Chironominae dorsal to the pedicels of the antennae and may be of diagnostic importance.

The mouthparts are strongly reduced (fig. 3A), functional mandibles having been observed in only one species, a podonomine from W. Australia (Downes & Colless 1967).   The *maxillary palps*, however, are usually well developed and have generally been considered to consist of 4 segments.   However, Saether (1971) points out that they are in fact 5 segmented, although the first segment may be small and poorly delimited from the rest of the maxilla.

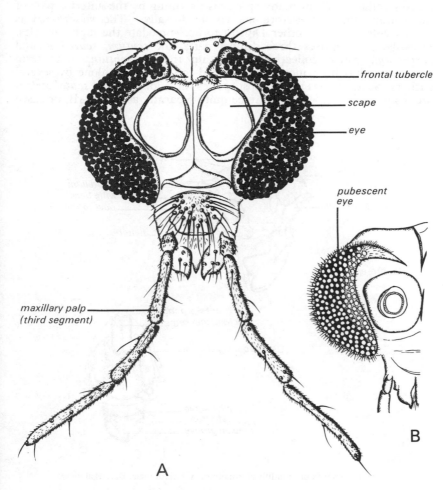

Fig. 3   A, anterior view of head of *Chironomus* sp. (antennae removed); B, part of the head of *Paracladius conversus* showing its pubescent eye.

The main subdivisions of the thorax are shown in figs 4A and 4B.   The
antepronotum (pronotum of most authors; see Saether (1971)) forms a
narrow collar which in many species is overhung by the anterior part of
the scutum and is therefore not visible dorsally.   The *mesothorax* is
greatly enlarged as in other Diptera to accommodate the flight muscles.
Dorsally, it comprises three distinct parts, the *scutum, scutellum* and
postnotum, which collectively make up the *mesonotum.*   The term
mesonotum has been incorrectly applied to the scutum alone by several
authors (Saether 1971).   In most species three longitudinal *scutal stripes*
are distinguishable.   They may be quite separate, as in fig. 4B, or fused

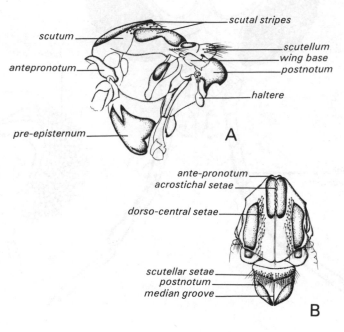

Fig. 4   Thorax of an adult chironomid: A, lateral view; B, dorsal view.

together.   In many species they are darker than the rest of the scutum but
in others the whole scutum is uniformly coloured and the stripes are then
difficult to discern.

In most species the postnotum possesses a median groove or keel, but
there is no trace of this in the marine Telmatogetoninae.

In the nomenclature of the wing venation I have followed Edwards (1929) and Coe (1950) in using the Comstock-Needham system (fig. 5). The cross-vein m-cu is lacking in the Chironominae and Orthocladiinae. Vein R_{2+3} is forked (fig. 5) only in the Tanypodinae and in many species is very faint or absent.

The wing membrane may be bare, or invested to varying degrees with macrotrichia (e.g. fig. 12C-D). On the other hand the wing margins and veins are usually fringed with macrotrichia which may lead the beginner to misinterpret a bare membrane as being sparsely clad with macrotrichia.

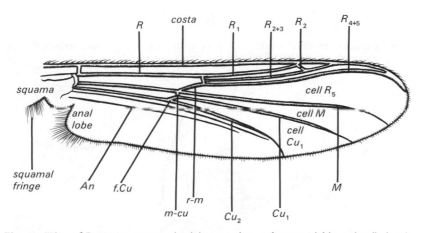

Fig. 5   Wing of *Psectrotanypus varius* (pigmentation and macrotrichia omitted) showing the terminology applied to the veins.

In a number of species the wings are distinctly marked, which may be due to differential distribution of pigment or of macrotrichia, or a combination of both.

The nomenclature of the leg segments is given in fig. 1. The *leg ratio* (length of the first tarsal segment divided by the length of the tibia) is often a useful diagnostic character. Similarly the *beard ratio* (length of longest tarsal seta divided by the diameter of the segment from which it arises) is sometimes helpful. Both ratios refer to the anterior legs unless the contrary is stated. The middle and posterior tibiae are usually equipped with distal spurs and combs the form of which may be of diagnostic importance. Examples from the three main subfamilies are shown in fig. 6. *Pulvilli* (pad-like processes beneath each claw) may be lacking but in some genera (e.g. *Psectrocladius*) they are well developed and conspicuous (fig. 7).

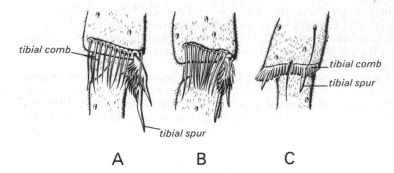

Fig. 6   Examples of tibial combs and spurs from each of the major subfamilies: A, Tanypodinae; B, Orthocladiinae; C, Chironominae.

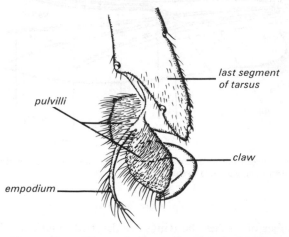

Fig. 7   Foot of *Psectrocladius* sp. showing large pulvilli.

The terminology applied to the various parts of the *hypopygium* (fig. 8) is somewhat confusing in that several names have sometimes been applied to the same structure.   Saether (1971) discussed this topic in some detail and his recommendations have largely been followed in this key.   The major appendages (fig. 8) are called *gonocoxite* and *gonostylus* to correspond with the terms coxite and style of Edwards (1929) and Coe (1950).   The names basistyle and dististyle have also been applied to these structures by a number of authors.   The terms *appendage 1* and *appendage 2* have, however, been retained for the lobes of the gonocoxite in the subfamily Chironominae, in preference to claspette and endomere as

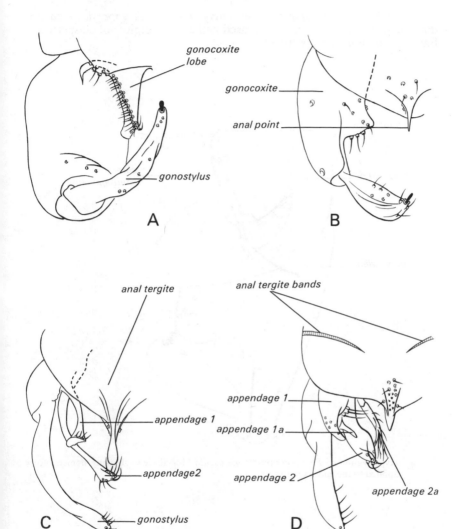

Fig. 8 Dorsal view of hypopygia of: A, *Arctopelopia griseipennis* (Tanypodinae); B, *Chaetocladius dissipatus* (Orthocladiinae); C, *Limnochironomus nervosus* (Chironomini); D, *Cladotanytarsus atridorsum* (Tanytarsini).

suggested by Saether (1971). Similarly, the names *appendage 1a* and *appendage 2a* (fig. 8D) have been used rather than digitus of claspette and digitus of endomere respectively.

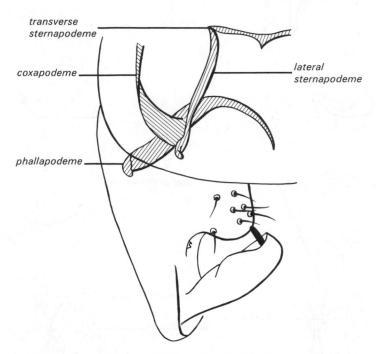

Fig. 9 Hypopygium of *Thienemanniella majuscula* (dorsal view) showing nomenclature applied to the endoskeleton.

Saether's (1971) recommendations have been followed with regard to the terminology applied to the endoskeleton of the hypopygium (fig. 9).

Characters other than those already mentioned have been used in a few isolated instances and explanations of these are given at the appropriate point in the key.

METHODS

Adult midges are most conveniently killed by immersion in 70% alcohol, which also acts as a suitable preservative, or by means of chloroform, amyl acetate or other volatile fluid. Many of the characters used in the key may be readily observed by examining the specimen immersed in alcohol under a low power dissecting microscope. For examination of fine detail, particularly of the hypopygium, it is necessary to dissect and mount the specimen on a microscope slide. A detailed technique for making a permanent preparation is described by Schlee (1966), but the following simplified version is adequate for most purposes. The hypopygium

Fig. 10   Slide of male midge, showing suggested arrangement of parts. (Crosses indicate fragments of coverslip used to raise the overlying coverslip).

should first be removed, using a pair of fine mounted needles, and placed in a hot (near boiling) 10% solution of caustic potash for about five minutes.   It should then be washed in distilled water and returned to 70% alcohol.   The complete specimen should be completely dehydrated by transferring through 90% to 100% alcohol.   The antennae, head, wings and legs should then be serially removed and mounted in euparal (obtainable from G.B.I. (Labs) Ltd., Heaton Mills, Heaton Street, Denton, Manchester) as indicated in fig. 10.   It is important that the wings should be flat and this is most easily achieved by placing them on the slide in a drop of alcohol, which is allowed to evaporate so that the wings become fixed to the slide, before adding the euparal and cover slip. It is also essential that the hypopygium should be mounted horizontally with the dorsal side uppermost and without being squashed. It is therefore necessary to raise the coverslip from the surface of the slide. For small species fragments of broken coverslip placed beneath the coverslip will suffice but for larger species short lengths of nylon fishing line, which is available in a wide range of diameters, have proved useful. The position of the hypopygium may then be adjusted by gently moving the coverslip.

The remainder of the abdomen should also be mounted with its dorsal surface uppermost. In some cases it is desirable to examine the dorsal setae of the thorax. In this case, it is necessary to slice off the top of the thorax using a sharp scalpel blade.

A useful alternative mounting medium to euparal is dimethyl hydantoin formaldehyde resin (Steedman 1958) which is available from Raymond A. Lamb, 6 Sunbeam Road, London NW10 6JL. This has the advantage that specimens can be mounted in it directly from 70% alcohol without further dehydration. Berlese fluid is also an excellent mounting medium and is in some ways superior to DMHF. Detailed instructions for its use are given by Disney (1975).

THE KEY

Volume 1 of the key is divided into sections corresponding with the various subfamilies. For ease and speed of identification the couplets have been kept as brief as possible, commensurate with accuracy, and as far as possible qualitative characters have been illustrated on the page facing the relevant couplet. Detailed drawings of hypopygia are contained in the second volume. Thus, having arrived at a name using Volume 1, the user may verify his diagnosis by reference to the appropriate figure in Volume 2. It is particularly important to confirm an identification in this way, since it is inevitable that from time to time the student will be confronted with a species not previously recorded from Britain and therefore not considered in the compilation of this key. The author would be grateful to receive details of any such records, particularly if they are accompanied by specimens, so that they can be incorporated into a future edition.

The user should bear in mind that the exact shape of hypopygial structures will appear to vary according to the angle at which they are viewed. Consequently it is stressed that care must be taken to ensure that hypopygia are mounted horizontally, dorsal side uppermost and without distortion through squashing.

In compiling this key, reference has been made to numerous works, including many recent revisions of genera. Acknowledgements of these are made at the appropriate point in the text.

A brief synonymy is given when the specific name used in the key differs from that used by Edwards (1929), Coe (1950) or Kloet & Hincks (1975). A detailed synonymy may be found in the work by Kloet & Hincks.

Data on distribution have not been included since the information available is so sparse as to be positively misleading. However, the author would be pleased to receive records of any species from anywhere in the British Isles, together with date of collection, national grid reference and brief habitat notes if possible, particularly if they are accompanied by specimens. If sufficient information is forthcoming in this way, distribution data may be included in a future edition of this key.

The author is also assembling a reference collection of named larvae with a view to compiling a key to larvae at some future date. Any reared adults, together with associated larval and pupal exuviae, would therefore be gratefully received.

TABLE 1   **The major subdivisions of the Chironomidae**

SUBFAMILY	TRIBE
TANYPODINAE	COELOTANYPODINI
	MACROPELOPIINI
	PENTANEURINI
	TANYPODINI
PODONOMINAE	
TELMATOGETONINAE	
DIAMESINAE	DIAMESINI
	PROTANYPINI
PRODIAMESINAE	
ORTHOCLADIINAE	METRIOCNEMINI
	ORTHOCLADIINI
CHIRONOMINAE	CHIRONOMINI
	TANYTARSINI

KEY TO SUBFAMILIES

1   Postnotum without a median groove or keel.   Antennal filament consisting of 6 segments (fig. 11A).   Marine—
TELMATOGETONINAE p. 38

—   Postnotum usually with a median groove or keel (except *Clunio*).   Antennal filament consisting of at least 10 segments. Mainly terrestrial or freshwater—   **2**

2   Cross-vein m-cu present (fig. 11B-D)—   **3**

—   Cross-vein m-cu absent—   **6**

3   Vein R_{2+3} present and simple (i.e. not forked) (fig. 11B-C).   Wing membrane bare.   Last antennal segment usually much longer than any of the preceding segments (except *Protanypus* in which a small incompletely separated terminal segment may be discernible)—   **4**

—   Vein R_{2+3} present and forked (fig. 11D) or absent.   Wing membrane often densely covered with macrotrichia.   Last antennal segment much shorter than penultimate segment—   **5**

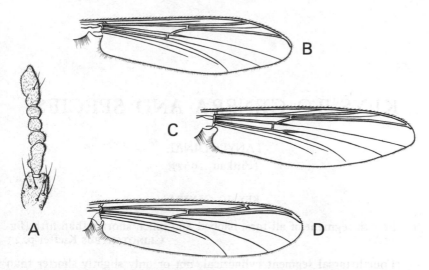

Fig. 11 A, antenna of *Psammathiomyia pectinata* (Telmatogetoninae); B-D, wings of:
B, *Potthastia gaedii* (Diamesinae); C, *Prodiamesa olivacea* (Prodiamesinae);
D, *Zavrelimyia nubila* (Tanypodinae).

4   f-Cu proximal to m-cu (fig. 11B)—   DIAMESINAE p. 38

—   f-Cu distal to m-cu (fig. 11C)—   PRODIAMESINAE p. 44

5(3) Vein R_{2+3} present and forked or absent. R_1 and R_{4+5} in close
      proximity (fig. 11D)—   TANYPODINAE p. 20

—   Vein R_{2+3} absent, R_1 and R_{4+5} well separated—
                                                      PODONOMINAE p. 38

6(2) Anterior leg ratio <1.0. Gonostylus bent inwards and usually with
      a distinct apical spine (e.g. fig. 8B)—   ORTHOCLADIINAE p. 45

—   Anterior leg ratio usually >1.0. Gonostylus usually directed
      backwards, rarely with a terminal spine (e.g. fig. 8C-D)—
                                                      CHIRONOMINAE p. 100

KEYS TO GENERA AND SPECIES

TANYPODINAE
(Fittkau, 1962)

KEY TO GENERA

1 Fourth segment of all tarsi bilobed and much shorter than fifth (fig. 12A)— CLINOTANYPUS Kieffer p. 27

— Fourth tarsal segment cylindrical, not or only slightly shorter than fifth— 2

2 Cross vein m-cu proximal to f.Cu (fig. 12B-C)— 3

— m-cu distal to f.Cu (fig. 12D)— 5

3 Distance between f.Cu and m-cu less than one third the length of Cu_1 (fig. 12B)— TANYPUS Meigen p. 36

— Distance between f.Cu and m-cu at least half the length of Cu_1 (fig. 12C)— 4

4 Wing membrane with macrotrichia, at least apically— PROCLADIUS Skuse p. 27

— Wing membrane lacking macrotrichia— PSILOTANYPUS Kieffer p. 28

5(2) Postnotum with a double row of long bristles medially (fig. 12E)— 6

— Postnotum bare— 9

6 Large pulvilli present (fig. 12F)— 7

— Pulvilli absent (fig. 12G)— 8

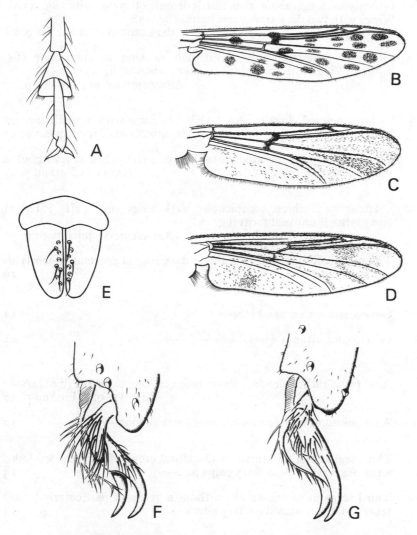

Fig. 12 A, terminal segments of tarsus of *Clinotanypus nervosus*; B-D, wings of: B, *Tanypus punctipennis*; C, *Procladius choreus*; D, *Macropelopia nebulosa*; E, postnotum of *Psectrotanypus varius*; F-G, foot of: F, *P. varius*; G, *M. nebulosa*.

7   Gonostylus long, about two thirds length of gonocoxite (fig. 13A).
    Wings with two dark transverse bands (fig. 13B)—
                                        PSECTROTANYPUS Kieffer p. 28

—   Gonostylus shorter, only about half as long as gonocoxite (fig.
    13C). Wings with three dark transverse bands (fig. 13D)—
                                        APSECTROTANYPUS Fittkau p. 27

8(6) Claws pointed distally (fig. 13E). Scutum with a small median
    hump (fig. 13F)—   MACROPELOPIA Thienemann p. 27

—   Claws broad and serrated distally (fig. 13G). Scutum without a
    median hump—   NATARSIA Fittkau p. 33

9(5) Tibiae with three conspicuous dark rings (fig. 13H). Tip of
    gonostylus of unusual form (fig. 13I)—
                                        ABLABESMYIA Johannsen p. 30

—   Tibiae unicolorous or with a single dark ring at one end. Gonostylus
    not as above—   10

10 Gonocoxite with a basal lobe—   11

—   Gonocoxite without a basal lobe—   15

11 Anal point rather slender, about twice as long as broad (fig. 14A)—
                                        XENOPELOPIA Fittkau p. 36

—   Anal point not well developed, broader than long—   12

12 Third segment of mid-tarsus with a distal group of strongly developed
    setae (fig. 14B). Maxillary palps pale—   13

—   Third segment of mid-tarsus without a group of particularly robust
    setae distally. Maxillary palps dark—   14

13 Scutum with a small median hump (cf. fig. 13F). Wings only faintly
    marked or not at all. Cross-veins pale—
                                        CONCHAPELOPIA Fittkau p. 32

—   Scutum without a median hump. Wings distinctly marked and with
    darkened cross-veins—   RHEOPELOPIA Fittkau p. 34

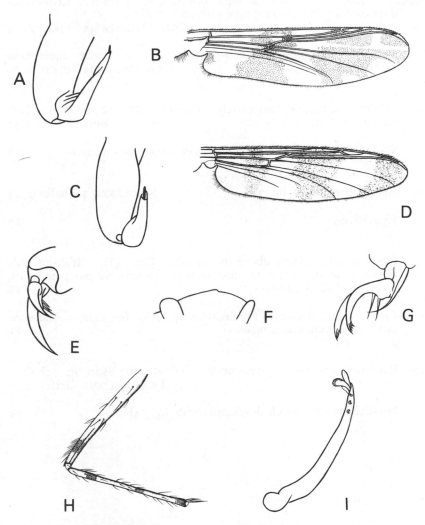

Fig. 13   A-B, *Psectrotanypus varius*: A, gonostylus; B, wing; C-D, *Apsectrotanypus trifascipennis*: C, gonostylus; D, wing; E-F, *Macropelopia notata*: E, claws; F, lateral view of thorax; G, claws of *Natarsia nugax*; H-I, *Ablabesmyia monilis*: H, femur and tibia; I, gonostylus.

14(12) Femora each with a dark brown ring apically. Cross-veins darkened and wing membrane with dark markings—
THIENEMANNIMYIA Fittkau p. 34

—   Femora unicolorous. Cross-veins pale and wing membrane unmarked—   ARCTOPELOPIA Fittkau p. 30

15(10) Wing membrane distinctively patterned with pale spots on a dark background (fig. 14C)—   GUTTIPELOPIA Fittkau p. 32

—   Wings unmarked or with dark areas on a pale background—   **16**

16   Eyes pubescent (cf. fig. 3B)—   NILOTANYPUS Kieffer p. 33

—   Eyes bare—   **17**

17   Costa usually ending above the tip of M (fig. 14D). If costa ends proximal to this point the abdomen is distinctively patterned with yellow and black bands—   **18**

—   Costa ending distinctly proximal to tip of M (fig. 14E). Abdomen not banded yellow and black—   **21**

18   Hind-tibiae without apical combs. Tibial spurs as in fig. 14F-G—
TRISSOPELOPIA Kieffer p. 36

—   Hind-tibiae with a well-developed comb (fig. 14H)—   **19**

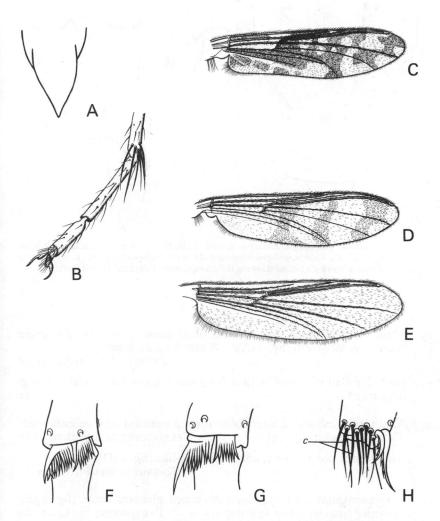

Fig. 14 A, anal point of *Xenopelopia nigricans*; B, tarsus of *Conchapelopia viator*; C-E, wings of: C, *Guttipelopia guttipennis*; D, *Zavrelimyia hirtimana*; E, *Paramerina cingulata*; F-G, tibial spurs of *Trissopelopia longimana*: F, posterior tibia; G, middle tibia; H, posterior tibial comb (c) and spurs of *Zavrelimyia hirtimana*.

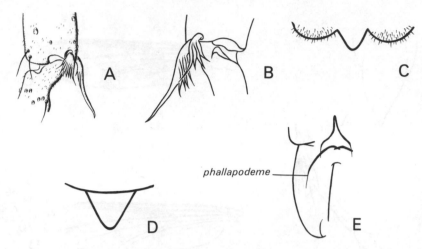

Fig. 15 A-B, tibial spurs of: A, *Zavrelimyia nubila*; B, *Krenopelopia binotata*; C-D, anal points of: C, *Telmatopelopia nemorum*; D, *Krenopelopia binotata*; E, gonocoxite of *Paramerina cingulata* showing the conspicuously darkened phallapodeme.

19 Main tooth of outer spur of hind tibial comb short, scarcely longer than accessory teeth (fig. 15A). Wings with dark markings—
ZAVRELIMYIA Fittkau p. 36

— Both hind tibial spurs with a long main tooth (fig. 15B). Wings unmarked— **20**

20 Anal tergite expanded laterally to form a rounded lobe on either side of the anal point (fig. 15C)— TELMATOPELOPIA Fittkau p. 34

— Anal tergite not as above, anal point peg-like (fig. 15D)—
KRENOPELOPIA Fittkau p. 32

21(17) Hypopygium with very long darkened phallapodemes (fig. 15E). Posterior tibia with two apical spurs— PARAMERINA Fittkau p. 34

— Phallapodemes not so conspicuous. Posterior tibia with a single spur, or spur completely lacking— **22**

22 Posterior tibia bearing a single apical spur—
MONOPELOPIA Fittkau p. 33

— Posterior tibia without a spur— LABRUNDINIA Fittkau p. 32

Tribe COELOTANYPODINI

Genus CLINOTANYPUS Kieffer

Only one species occurs in the British Isles, readily recognizable by the very short, bilobed, fourth tarsal segment (fig. 12A). The hypopygium is shown in fig. 77A—
Clinotanypus nervosus (Meigen)

Tribe MACROPELOPIINI

Genus APSECTROTANYPUS Fittkau

There is only one European representative of this genus which should be easily identified from the characters given in the key to genera. The wing is shown in fig. 13D and the hypopygium in fig. 77B—   **Apsectrotanypus trifascipennis** (Zetterstedt)

Genus MACROPELOPIA Thienemann

1   Cross-vein r-m darkened, wing otherwise unmarked.   Hypopygium as in fig. 77D—   **Macropelopia goetghebueri** (Kieffer)

—   Wing membrane with distinct dark markings (fig. 16A-B)—   **2**

2   Gonocoxite with a small lobe (fig. 16C).   Wing as in fig. 16B. Hypopygium fig. 77C—   **M. notata** (Meigen)

—   Gonocoxite without a lobe.   Wing as in fig. 16A.   Hypopygium fig. 78A—   **M. nebulosa** (Meigen)

Genus PROCLADIUS Skuse

1   Gonostylus without a posterior process (fig. 16D).   Hypopygium fig. 78C—   **Procladius simplicistilus** Freeman

—   Gonostylus with a distinct posterior process (fig. 16E-G)—   **2**

2   Length of posterior process of gonostylus at least 3 times its diameter
     (fig. 16F-G).   Abdomen black—   3

—   Length of posterior process of gonostylus no more than twice its
     diameter (e.g. fig. 16E).   Abdominal tergites pale posteriorly—   4

3   Phallapodeme with a cluster of small 'teeth' distally (fig. 16H).
     Hypopygium fig. 78D—   **Procladius signatus** (Zetterstedt)

—   Phallapodeme simple.   Hypopygium fig. 78B—
                                       P. crassinervis (Zetterstedt)

4(2) Posterior process of gonocoxite scarcely as long as broad.   Wing
     without a dark shade over distal half.   Hypopygium fig. 79A—
                                       P. sagittalis (Kieffer)

—   Posterior process of gonocoxite about twice as long as broad (fig.
     16E).   Wing with a dark shade over distal half (best seen in a fresh
     specimen).   Hypopygium fig. 79C—   **P. choreus** (Meigen)

I am unable to separate *P. choreus* (Meig.) sensu Coe 1950, from *P. culiciformis* (L.) sensu
Coe (fig. 79B).

Genus PSECTROTANYPUS Kieffer

Only one species of this genus is known from the British Isles.   The
characters given in the key to genera should suffice to identify
it.   The wing is shown in fig. 13B and the hypopygium in fig. 79D—
                              Psectrotanypus varius (Fabricius)

Genus PSILOTANYPUS Kieffer

1   Gonostylus (fig. 16I) with a pronounced internal swelling and a short
     posterior process.   Background colour of scutum yellowish.
     Hypopygium fig. 79E—   **Psilotanypus rufovittatus** (van der Wulp)

—   Gonostylus not as above, thorax black—   2

2   Posterior margin of gonostylus abruptly angled (fig. 16J).
     Hypopygium fig. 80A—   **P. lugens** (Kieffer)

—   Posterior margin of gonostylus smoothly rounded (fig. 16K).
     Hypopygium fig. 80B—   **P. flavifrons** (Edwards)

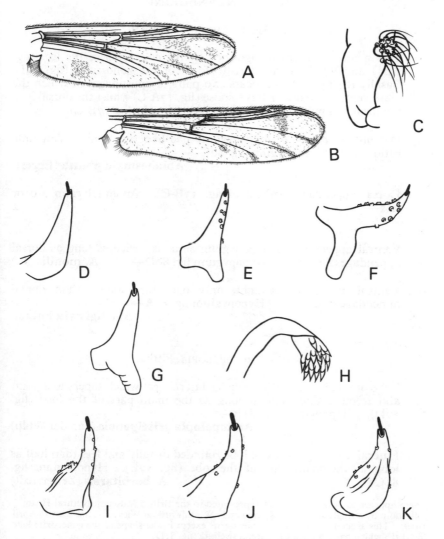

Fig. 16   A–B, wings of: A, *Macropelopia nebulosa*; B, *M. notata*; C, gonocoxite of *M. notata*; D–G, gonostylus of: D, *Procladius simplicistilus*; E, *P. choreus*; F, *P. signatus*; G, *P. crassinervis*; H, phallapodeme of *P. signatus*; I–K, gonostylus of: I, *Psilotanypus rufovittatus*; J, *P. lugens*; K, *P. flavifrons*.

Tribe PENTANEURINI

Genus ABLABESMYIA Johannsen

This genus is easily distinguished by the coloration of the legs (fig. 13H) and by the characteristic form of the gonostylus (fig. 13I). Basally the hypopygium bears two pairs of appendages of which the more ventral is more or less spinose (fig. 17A-C) whilst the dorsal is in the form of a pubescent pad (fig. 17A) or brush (fig. 17B-C).

I   Dorsal appendage of hypopygium pad-like (fig. 17A). Antennal ratio *c*. 2·5. Hypopygium fig. 80C—
Ablabesmyia phatta (Eggert)

—   Dorsal appendage brush-like (fig. 17B-C). Antennal ratio 2·0 or less—   **2**

2   Ventral appendage of hypopygium sinuous, twice as long as dorsal appendage (fig. 17B). Hypopygium fig. 80D—   **A. monilis** (L.)

—   Ventral appendage straight, only one third longer than dorsal appendage (fig. 17C). Hypopygium fig. 81A—
A. longistyla Fittkau

Genus ARCTOPELOPIA Fittkau

I   Lobe of gonocoxite with a slender lateral arm which tapers to a point and is more than half as long as the main part of the lobe (fig. 17D). Hypopygium fig. 81B—
Arctopelopia griseipennis (van der Wulp)

—   Lateral arm of gonocoxite lobe rounded distally and less than half as long as the main part of the lobe (fig. 17E). Hypopygium fig. 81C—   **A. barbitarsis** (Zetterstedt)

There appears to be a third species represented in the British Museum (Natural History) collection, by a single specimen collected by F. W. Edwards at Wicken, Cambs. on 26 April 1916.   This specimen resembles *A. barbitarsis* except in the shape of the gonocoxite lobe (fig. 17F) which has a pronounced lateral swelling (fig. 81D).

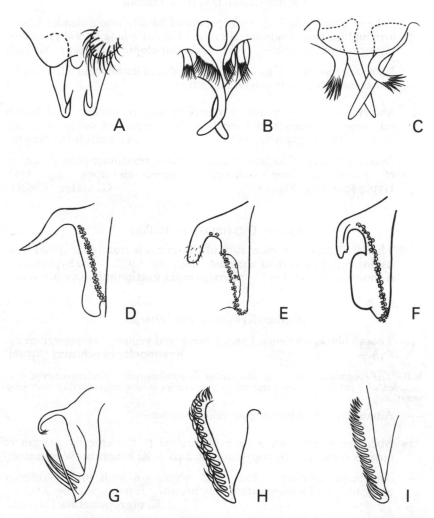

Fig. 17 A-C, basal appendages of hypopygium (dorsal view) of; A, *Ablabesmyia phatta*; B, *A. monilis*; C, *A. longistyla*; D-I, basal gonocoxite lobes of: D, *Arctopelopia griseipennis*; E, *A. barbitarsis*; F, *Arctopelopia* sp. a; G, *Conchapelopia melanops*; H, *C. pallidula*; I, *C. viator*.

Genus CONCHAPELOPIA Fittkau

1   Lobe of gonocoxite (fig. 17G) produced basally into a slender lateral arm and bearing a sub-apical group of about 5 long lateral processes. Hypopygium fig. 82A—   **Conchapelopia melanops** (Meigen)

—   Lobe of gonocoxite (fig. 17H-I) not produced basally and with shorter processes along entire lateral margin—   **2**

2   Abdominal tergites 7 and 8 mostly brown, remainder of abdomen yellowish.   Processes of gonocoxite lobe expanded subapically (fig. 17H).   Hypopygium fig. 82B—   **C. pallidula** (Meigen)

—   Anterior halves of tergites 7 and 8 brown, remainder pale. Processes of gonocoxite lobe uniformly tapered to apex (fig. 17I). Hypopygium fig. 82C—   **C. viator** (Kieffer)

Genus GUTTIPELOPIA Fittkau

The sole British representative of this genus is readily identified from its distinctive pattern of wing markings (fig. 14C).   The hypopygium is shown in fig. 82D—   **Guttipelopia guttipennis** (van der Wulp)

Genus KRENOPELOPIA Fittkau

1   Thorax black, abdomen banded black and yellow.   Hypopygium fig. 83A—   **Krenopelopia schineri** (Strobl)

N.B. The systematic position of this species is problematical.   For convenience it is included with the *Krenopelopia* spp. which it resembles in most respects other than wing venation.

—   Almost entirely white or pale yellow species—   **2**

2   Abdomen white with a dark fleck close to the anterior margin of tergites 6 and 7.   Hypopygium fig. 83B— **K. binotata** (Wiedemann)

—   Abdominal tergites 1 and 2 all white, 3-6 with brown anterior margins, 7 and 8 more extensively brown.   Hypopygium fig. 83C— **K. nigropunctata** (Staeger)

Genus LABRUNDINIA Fittkau

The single British species is characterized by its small size (wing length 1·5-2·0 mm) and the absence of spurs on the posterior tibiae.   The hypopygium is shown in fig. 83D—
                              Labrundinia longipalpis (Goetghebuer)

Genus MONOPELOPIA Fittkau

Only one British species is referred here. It is a small species (wing length 2·0-2·5 mm) differing from *Labrundinia* in the possession of a short posterior tibial spur. The hypopygium is shown in fig. 84A—

Monopelopia tenuicalcar (Kieffer)
(*Pentaneura ferrugineicollis* (Mg.), Edwards 1929)
(*Pentaneura brevitibialis* Goetghebuer, Coe 1950)

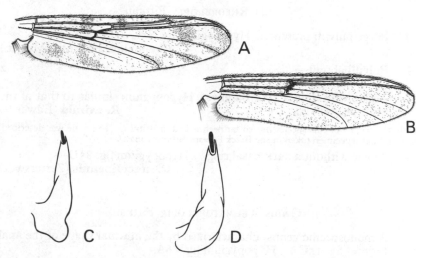

Fig. 18 A-B, wings of: A, *Natarsia punctata*; B, *N. nugax*; C-D, gonostyli of: C, *N. punctata*; D, *N. nugax*.

Genus NATARSIA Fittkau

1 Wings with conspicuous dark markings (fig. 18A). Gonostylus (fig. 18C) swollen basally. Hypopygium fig. 84B—
Natarsia punctata (Fabricius)

— Wings unmarked except for a dark fleck around the cross-veins (fig. 18B). Gonostylus rounded basally (fig. 18D). Hypopygium fig. 84C—
N. nugax (Walker)

Genus NILOTANYPUS Kieffer

The only British representative of this genus is easily identified by virtue of its pubescent eyes (cf. fig. 3B) and small size (wing length 1·5-2·0 mm). Hypopygium as in fig. 84D—
Nilotanypus dubius (Meigen)

Genus PARAMERINA Fittkau

1   Abdominal tergites 2 and 5 pale.   Hypopygium as in fig. 85A—
                                          Paramerina divisa (Walker)

—   Tergites 2 and 5 mainly brown but with narrowly pale anterior
    margins.   Hypopygium fig. 85B—   **P. cingulata** (Walker)

Genus RHEOPELOPIA Fittkau

1   Large pulvilli present.   Hypopygium fig. 85C—
                                          Rheopelopia ornata (Meigen)

—   Pulvilli absent—   2

2   Tibiae with a dark ring basally.   Hypopygium similar to that of the
    next species—   **R. eximia** (Edwards)

Only the female of this species has so far been found in Britain.   The male was described
from a single specimen taken in the Black Forest (Fittkau 1962).

—   Tibiae without a dark basal ring.   Hypopygium fig. 85D—
                                          R. maculipennis (Zetterstedt)

Genus TELMATOPELOPIA Fittkau

A monospecific genus, characterized by the unusual shape of the anal
tergite (fig. 15C).   Hypopygium fig. 86A—
                                Telmatopelopia nemorum (Goetghebuer)

Genus THIENEMANNIMYIA Fittkau

1   Bases of tibiae and tips of femora each with a dark ring—   2

—   Tibial bases not ringed.   Femora ringed or not—   3

2   Anterior margin of third abdominal tergite with three dark spots (fig.
    19B) which may be fused to form a continuous band.   Hypopygium
    fig. 86B—   **Thienemannimyia lentiginosa** (Fries)

—   Anterior margin of third abdominal tergite with a pair of dark spots
    only (fig. 19A).   Hypopygium fig. 86C—   **T. laeta** (Meigen)

3(1) Tips of femora with a dark ring.   Hypopygium fig. 86D—
                                          T. woodi (Edwards)

—   Femora without dark apical rings—   4

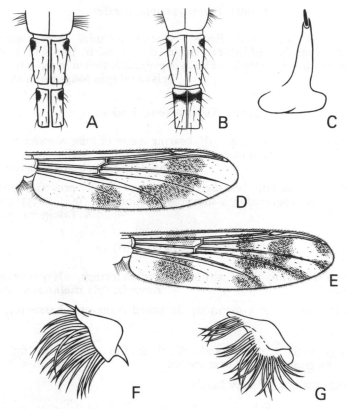

Fig. 19   A-B, anterior abdominal tergites of: A, *Thienemannimyia laeta*; B, *T. lentiginosa*; C, gonostylus of *T. fusciceps*; D-E, wings of: D, *T. carnea*; E, *T. northumbrica*; F-G, basal lobes of gonocoxite of: F, *Xenopelopia nigricans*; G, *X. falcigera*.

4   Gonostylus with a short posterior process (fig. 19C).   Hypopygium
    fig. 87A—   **T. fusciceps** (Edwards)

—   Gonostylus lacking such a process—   5

5   Dark markings on wing membrane confined to the area distal to the
    cross-veins (fig. 19D).   Hypopygium fig. 87B—
                                                T. carnea (Fabricius)

—   Dark markings also present proximal to cross-veins (fig. 19E).
    Hypopygium fig. 87C—   **T. northumbrica** (Edwards)

Genus TRISSOPELOPIA Kieffer

There is only one British species included here, which is predominantly reddish-brown in colour with the scutal stripes scarcely differentiated. The hypopygium is shown in fig. 87D—

Trissopelopia longimana (Staeger)

Genus XENOPELOPIA Fittkau

1   Lobe of gonocoxite (fig. 19F) bearing a row of long, slender processes along entire median margin. Hypopygium fig. 88A—

Xenopelopia nigricans (Goetghebuer)

—   Lobe of gonocoxite bearing two groups of slender processes medially, which are separated by a short bare section (fig. 19G). Hypopygium fig. 88B—

X. falcigera (Kieffer)

Genus ZAVRELIMYIA Fittkau

1   Wings uniformly dark, without distinct markings. Hypopygium fig. 88C—

Zavrelimyia melanura (Meigen)

—   Wings with 2 or 3 distinctly darkened transverse bands (fig. 20A-C)—

2

2   Wings with 3 dark bands distal to the cross-veins (fig. 20A). Hypopygium as in the next species—

Z. hirtimana (Kieffer)

—   Wings with only 2 dark bands

3

3   Tip of vein Cu_2 surrounded by a separate dark field (fig. 20B). Hypopygium fig. 88D—

Z. barbatipes (Kieffer)

—   Area surrounding tip of vein Cu_2 pale (fig. 20C). Hypopygium fig. 89A—

Z. nubila (Meigen)

Tribe TANYPODINI

Genus TANYPUS Meigen

1   Wing membrane with numerous dark spots (fig. 20D). Hypopygium fig. 89B—

Tanypus punctipennis Meigen

—   Cross-veins and adjacent wing membrane dark, wing otherwise unmarked (fig. 20E). Hypopygium fig. 89C—

T. vilipennis (Kieffer)

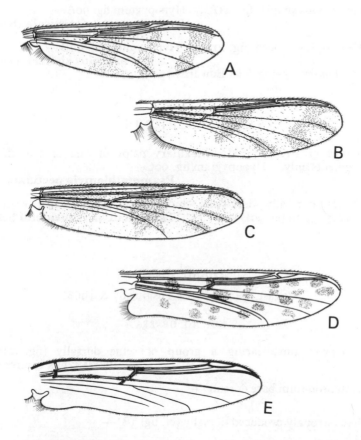

Fig. 20   A-E, wings of: A, *Zavrelimyia hirtimana*: B, *Z. barbatipes*; C, *Z. nubila*; D, *Tanypus punctipennis*; E, *T. vilipennis* (macrotrichia are present on the membrane of both *Tanypus* spp. but have been omitted from the drawing.).

PODONOMINAE

1   Gonostylus simple (fig. 21A).   Hypopygium fig. 90A—
Lasiodiamesa sphagnicola (Kieffer)

—   Gonostylus bilobed (fig. 21B).   Hypopygium fig. 90B—
Parochlus kiefferi (Garrett)
(Podonomus peregrinus Edwards 1929)

TELMATOGETONINAE

1   Wings greatly reduced.   Maxillary palps of one or two distinct
segments only.   Hypopygium fig. 90C—
Psammathiomyia pectinata Deby

—   Wings normally developed, palps with four distinct segments.
Hypopygium fig. 90D—   **Thalassomyia frauenfeldi** Schiner

DIAMESINAE

(Pagast 1947.   Serra-Tosio 1967 & 1968)

KEY TO GENERA

1   Antepronotum bearing a group of setae dorsally (fig. 21C)—
PROTANYPUS Kieffer p. 40

—   Antepronotum bare dorsally—   2

2   Eyes strongly produced dorsally (cf. fig. 3B)—   3

—   Eyes not, or scarcely, produced dorsally—   4

3   Hypopygium with an anal point (fig. 21D)—
PSEUDODIAMESA Goetghebuer p. 44

—   Anal point absent—   SYNDIAMESA Kieffer p. 44

4(2)   Wing membrane with microtrichia (visible at ×200 magni-
fication)—   5

—   Wing membrane without microtrichia—   POTTHASTIA Kieffer p. 42

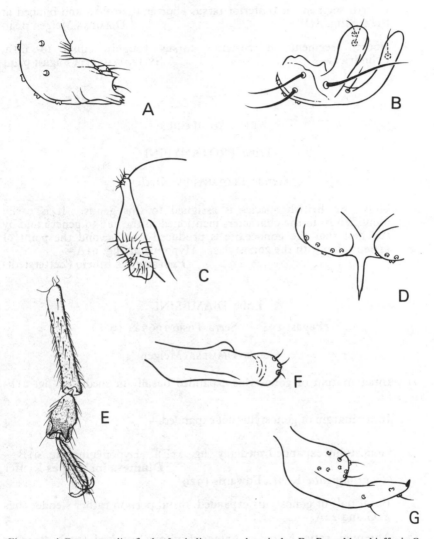

Fig. 21   A-B, gonostyli of: A, *Lasiodiamesa sphagnicola*; B, *Parochlus kiefferi*; C, antepronotum of *Protanypus morio*; D, anal point of *Pseudosmittia branickii*; E, distal tarsal segments of *Diamesa cinerella*; F-G, gonostyli of: F, *D. insignipes*; G, *D. tonsa*.

5   Fourth segment of posterior tarsus shorter than fifth and bilobed at
    the tip (fig. 21E)—   DIAMESA Meigen p. 40

—   Fourth segment of posterior tarsus roughly equal to fifth,
    cylindrical—   SYMPOTTHASTIA Pagast p. 44

KEYS TO SPECIES

Tribe PROTANYPINI

Genus PROTANYPUS Kieffer

Only one British species is assigned to this genus. It is easily
identified from the characters mentioned in the key to genera and by
the fact that the gonocoxite is produced well beyond the point of
articulation with the gonostylus. Hypopygium fig. 91A—
                              Protanypus morio (Zetterstedt)

Tribe DIAMESINI

(Pagast 1947.   Serra-Tosio 1967 & 1968)

Genus DIAMESA Meigen

1   Inner margin of gonostylus expanded basally or medially (fig. 21F-
    G)—   **2**

—   Inner margin of gonostylus not expanded—   **4**

2   Gonostylus expanded medially (fig. 21F).   Hypopygium fig. 91B—
                              Diamesa insignipes Kieffer
    (*D. prolongata* Kieff., Edwards 1929)

—   Basal half of gonostylus expanded, distal portion rather slender (figs
    21G and 22A)—   **3**

3   Antennal ratio *c.* 0·3.   Antennal plume reduced, each flagellar
    segment bearing a single whorl of short setae.   Hypopygium fig.
    91C—   **D. tonsa** (Walker)
    (*D. culicoides* Heeger, Edwards 1929)

—   Antennal ratio >0·5.   Antennal plume normally developed.
    Hypopygium fig. 92A—   **D. thienemanni** Kieffer

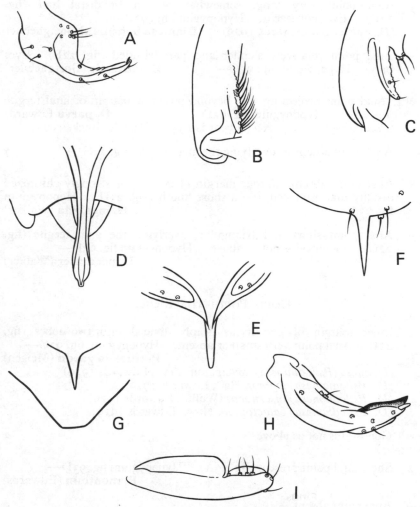

Fig. 22 A, gonostylus of *Diamesa thienemanni*; B–C, gonocoxites of: B, *D. bohemani*; C, *D. latitarsis*; D–G, anal points of: D, *D. bohemani*; E, *D. latitarsis*; F, *D. parva*; G, *D. permacer*; H–I, gonostyli of: H, *D. incallida*; I, *Potthastia gaedii*.

4(1) Gonocoxite with one or two long finger-like lobes (fig. 22B – C)—— 5

— Gonocoxite not as above 6

5   Anal point very long, somewhat swollen in distal half (fig. 22D). Eyes pubescent. Hypopygium fig. 92B—
(*D. waltli* Mg., Edwards 1929)   **Diamesa bohemani** Goetghebuer

—   Anal point relatively slender and parallel-sided (fig. 22E). Eyes bare. Hypopygium fig. 92C—   **D. latitarsis** (Goetghebuer)

6(4) Anal point projecting well beyond posterior margin of anal tergite (fig. 22F). Hypopygium fig. 92D—   **D. parva** Edwards
(*Pseudokiefferiella parva* (Edwards 1932), Kloet & Hincks 1975)

—   Anal point absent or overlying the anal tergite (fig. 22G)—   7

7   Anal point absent. Inner margin of gonostylus strongly chitinized distally and produced into a short 'tooth' (fig. 22H). Hypopygium fig. 93A—   **D. incallida** (Walker)

—   Anal point short and triangular, overlying the anal tergite (fig. 22G). Gonostylus not as above. Hypopygium fig. 93B—
D. permacer (Walker)

Genus POTTHASTIA Kieffer

1   Inner margin of gonostylus deeply divided into two lobes (fig. 22I). Anal point very small or absent. Hypopygium fig. 93C—
Potthastia gaedii (Meigen)
(*Diamesa (Psilodiamesa) lacteipennis* Zett., Edwards 1929)
(*D. (Psilodiamesa) ammon* Hal., Edwards 1929)
(*D. (Psilodiamesa) inscendens* (Walk.), Edwards 1929)
(*D. (Psilodiamesa) galactoptera* Now., Edwards 1929)

—   Gonostylus not as above—   2

2   Short anal point present (fig. 23A). Hypopygium fig. 93D—
P. montium (Edwards)

—   Anal point absent—   3

3   All wing veins pale. In fresh specimens the scutal stripes are dull black, the whole thorax with a whitish bloom. Hypopygium fig. 94A—   **P. longimana** Kieffer
(*Diamesa (Psilodiamesa) campestris* (Edwards 1929))

—   Anterior veins blackish. In fresh specimens the scutal stripes are shining black. Hypopygium fig. 94B—   **P. pastoris** (Edwards)

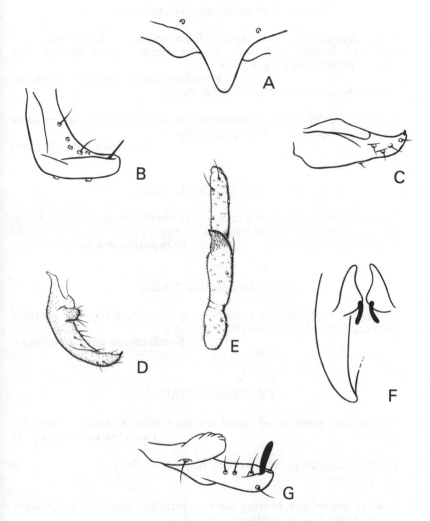

Fig. 23 A, anal point of *Potthastia montium*; B-D, gonostyli of: B, *Pseudodiamesa branickii*; C, *P. nivosa*; D, *Syndiamesa edwardsi*; E, distal segments of maxillary palp of *Odontomesa fulva*; F-G, *Prodiamesa olivacea*; F, ventro-basal appendages of hypopygium; G, gonostylus.

Genus PSEUDODIAMESA Goetghebuer

1 Wing membrane with macrotrichia distally. Gonostylus not thickened basally and with a long slender spine distally (fig. 23B). Hypopygium fig. 94C—

Pseudodiamesa branickii (Nowicki)
(Syndiamesa pilosa Kieff., Edwards 1929)

— Wing membrane bare. Gonostylus thickened basally, apical spine very short (fig. 23C). Hypopygium fig. 95A—

P. nivosa (Goetghebuer)

Genus SYMPOTTHASTIA Pagast

Only one species is referred here. The characters given in the key to genera, together with the figure of its hypopygium (fig. 95B) should suffice to identify it— **Sympotthastia zavreli** Pagast

Genus SYNDIAMESA Kieffer

This genus contains only one British species which is easily identified from the form of the gonostylus (fig. 23D)—

Syndiamesa edwardsi Pagast

PRODIAMESINAE

1 Penultimate segment of maxillary palp with a distal 'tooth' (fig. 23E)— ODONTOMESA Pagast p. 45

— Penultimate segment of maxillary palp not toothed— 2

2 Base of gonocoxite bearing darkly chitinized elongate appendages, arising from obvious swellings (fig. 23F)— PRODIAMESA Kieffer p. 45

— Basal appendages of gonocoxite pale, not arising from obvious swellings— MONODIAMESA Kieffer p. 45

Genus MONODIAMESA Kieffer

Only one species of this genus has been recorded from the British Isles. It is easily recognized from the characters mentioned in the key to genera and by its characteristic hypopygium (fig. 95C)—
Monodiamesa bathyphila (Kieffer)

Genus ODONTOMESA Pagast

A monospecific genus, characterized by the presence of a distal tooth on the penultimate segment of the maxillary palp (fig. 23E). The hypopygium is also distinctive (fig. 95D)—
Odontomesa fulva (Kieffer)

Genus PRODIAMESA Kieffer

1 Gonostylus bilobed (fig. 23G).   Hypopygium fig. 96A—
Prodiamesa olivacea (Meigen)

— Gonostylus simple.   Hypopygium fig. 96B—
P. rufovittata Goetghebuer

ORTHOCLADIINAE

(Brundin 1956)

KEY TO GENERA

1 Postnotum without a median groove or keel.   Marine—
CLUNIO Haliday p. 82

— Postnotum with a median longitudinal groove or keel—   2

2 Wing membrane with macrotrichia, apically at least—   3

— Wing membrane quite bare—   11

3 Gonostylus bifurcate (fig. 24A-B)—   4

— Gonostylus simple—   5

4 Outer ramus of gonostylus with several long robust setae (fig. 24A)—
EURYCNEMUS van der Wulp p. 66

— Gonostylus without such setae (fig. 24B)— BRILLIA Kieffer p. 54

5(3) Eyes pubescent (cf. fig. 3B)— THIENEMANNIA Kieffer p. 98

— Eyes bare— 6

6 Vein Cu_2 strongly curved (e.g. fig. 24C)— 7

— Vein Cu_2 almost straight or very slightly curved (e.g. fig. 24D)— 9

7 Anal point minute or absent—
GYMNOMETRIOCNEMUS Goetghebuer p. 86

— Anal point well developed— 8

8 Vein R_{4+5} ending above tip of Cu_1(fig. 24E)—
PARAMETRIOCNEMUS Goetghebuer p. 92

— Vein R_{4+5} ending distinctly proximal to tip of Cu_1 (fig. 24C)—
PARAPHAENOCLADIUS Sparck & Thienemann p. 92

9(6) Anal tergite very small, triangular, anal point weakly developed (fig. 24F)— HETEROTANYTARSUS Sparck p. 67

— Anal tergite normally developed with a distinct anal point— 10

10 Costa ending abruptly at tip of vein R_{4+5} (fig. 24G)—
HETEROTRISSOCLADIUS (Sparck) p. 67

— Costa strongly produced beyong R_{4+5}—
METRIOCNEMUS van der Wulp p. 89

11(2) Veins R_1 and R_{4+5} fused with the thickened costa (fig.. 24H)— 12

— Veins R_1 and R_{4+5} separate from the costa as usual— 13

12 Posterior tibia strongly expanded distally (fig. 25A)—
CORYNONEURA Winnertz p. 84

— Posterior tibia cylindrical— THIENEMANNIELLA Kieffer p. 98

13(11) Fourth segment of each tarsus bilobed, much shorter than the fifth segment— CARDIOCLADIUS Kieffer p. 56

— Fourth segment of each tarsus cylindrical, usually as long as, or longer than the fifth— 14

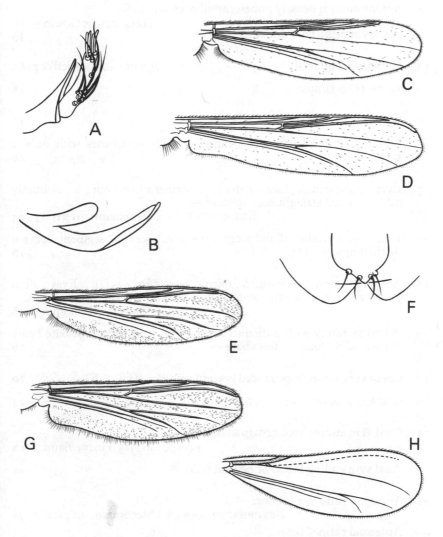

Fig. 24   A-B, gonostyli of: A, *Eurycnemus crassipes*; B, *Brillia longifurca*; C-E, wings of:
C, *Paraphaenocladius impensus*; D, *Metriocnemus hygropetricus*, E,
Parametriocnemus stylatus; F, anal tergite of *Heterotanytarsus apicalis*; G-H,
wings of: G, *Heterotrissocladius marcidus*; H, *Corynoneura scutellata*.

14 Antepronotum densely pubescent all over (fig. 25B)—
HELENIELLA Gowin p. 86
— Antepronotum bare dorsally— **15**

15 Gonostylus bilobed (fig. 25C)— DIPLOCLADIUS Kieffer p. 64
— Gonostylus simple— **16**

16 Squama (fig. 5) bare— **17**
— Squama at least partially fringed, though sometimes with only 2 setae— **26**

17 Eyes pubescent. Last antennal segment without a distinctly differentiated straight seta apically—
EUKIEFFERIELLA Thienemann (in part) p. 64
— Eyes usually bare; if pubescent, the last antennal segment bears a distinct apical seta (fig. 25D)— **18**

18 Antenna with a distinct apical seta (fig. 25D). Eyes often pubescent. Gonocoxite with a single median lobe—
SMITTIA Holmgren p. 96
— Antenna rarely with a distinct apical seta; if so the gonocoxite bears three median lobes. Eyes bare— **19**

19 Costa very strongly produced beyond vein R_{4+5} (fig. 25E)— **20**
— Costa not, or only weakly, produced (fig. 25F)— **24**

20 Anal vein ending well proximal to f.Cu—
KRENOSMITTIA Thienemann p. 86
— Anal vein ending below or beyond f.Cu— **21**

21 Antennal ratio 1·2 or more—
BRYOPHAENOCLADIUS Thienemann (in part) p. 78
— Antennal ratio <1·0— **22**

22 Gonocoxite bearing two lobes (fig. 25G). Marine—
THALASSOSMITTIA Strenzke p. 96
— Gonocoxite with only one lobe. Terrestrial or freshwater species— **23**

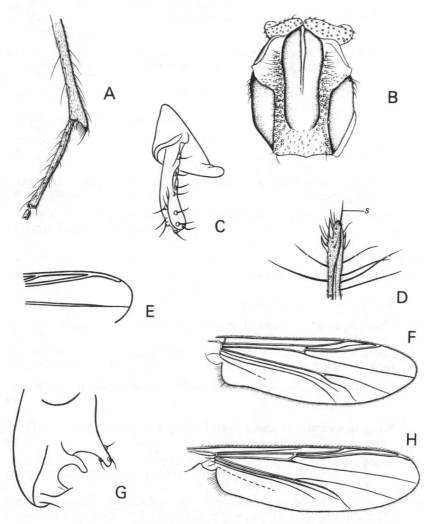

Fig. 25   A, tip of tibia and first tarsal segment of *Corynoneura scutellata*; B, dorsal view of scutum and antepronotum of *Heleniella ornaticollis*; C, gonostylus of *Diplocladius cultriger*; D, tip of antenna of *Smittia leucopogon*; E, wing-tip of *Krenosmittia camptophleps*, showing produced costa; F, wing of *Camptocladius stercorarius*; G, gonocoxite of *Thalassosmittia thalassophila*; H, wing of *Epoicocladius flavens*.

23 Vein R_{2+3} ending at, or before, midway between veins R_1 and R_{4+5}. Tip of R_{4+5} above or scarcely proximal to tip of Cu_1 (fig. 25H)— EPOICOCLADIUS Zavrel p. 86

— Vein R_{2+3} ending close to vein R_{4+5} or fused with it. Tip of R_{4+5} well proximal to tip of Cu_1— PARAKIEFFERIELLA Thienemann p. 92

24(19) Vein R_{4+5} ending above or beyond tip of Cu_1. Last segment of each tarsus flattened dorso-ventrally— ACAMPTOCLADIUS Brundin p. 78

— Vein R_{4+5} ending distinctly proximal to Cu_1. Apical tarsal segments cylindrical— **25**

25 Anal vein very long, reaching almost to wing margin (fig. 25F). Pulvilli present— CAMPTOCLADIUS van der Wulp p. 80

— Anal vein ending well before wing margin. Pulvilli absent— PSEUDOSMITTIA Goetghebuer p. 94

26(16) Eyes bare— **27**

— Eyes pubescent (cf. fig. 3B)— **39**

27 Vein Cu_2 strongly curved (cf. fig. 24C)— **28**

— Vein Cu_2 nearly straight or only weakly curved (cf. fig. 24D)— **32**

28 Costa not produced beyond R_{4+5}. Anal tergite swollen medially to form a longitudinal ridge (fig. 26A)— MESOSMITTIA Brundin p. 89

— Costa produced, usually very distinctly. Anal tergite not as above— **29**

29 Wing membrane coarsely dotted with microtrichia ($\times200$) (cf. fig. 26F)— **30**

— Wing membrane only very finely punctate ($\times200$)— PSEUDORTHOCLADIUS Goetghebuer p. 94

30 Anal point broad and pubescent (fig. 26B-C) or lacking. Scutum often bearing scale-like setae (fig. 26D)— LIMNOPHYES Eaton p. 88

— Anal point always present and bare. Thorax bearing simple setae only— **31**

31 Anterior leg ratio at least 0·6— BRYOPHAENOCLADIUS Thienemann (in part) p. 78

— Anterior leg ratio <0·5— PARALIMNOPHYES Brundin p. 92

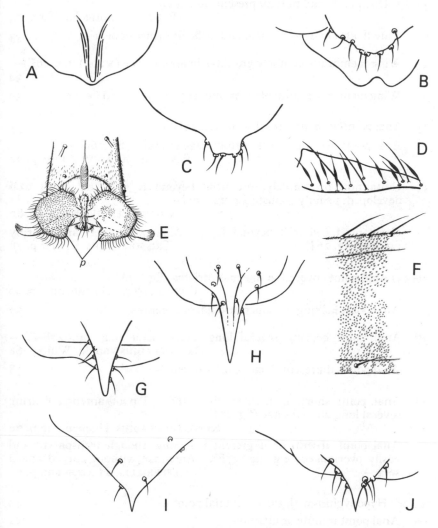

Fig. 26   A–C, anal tergites of: A, *Mesosmittia flexuella*; B, *Limnophyes truncorum*; C,
L. habilis; D, prescutellar setae of *L. prolongatus*; E, ventral view of foot of
Psectrocladius sp. (*p* = pulvilli); F, portion of wing membrane of *Chaetocladius
perennis*; G-J, anal points of; G, *Paratrissocladius excerptus*; H, *Chaetocladius
piger*; I, *C. dentiforceps*; J, *Trissocladius brevipalpis*.

32(27) Distinct, broad pulvilli present (fig. 26E)—
                              PSECTROCLADIUS Kieffer p. 74
—   Pulvilli absent or very small and difficult to distinguish—   33

33   Wing membrane coarsely granular in appearance (×200) (fig. 26F)—
                                                                   34
—   Wing membrane quite plain or only very finely dotted (×200)—   36

34   Anal point without lateral setae (fig. 26H,J)—   35
—   Anal point bearing several strong setae laterally (fig. 26G)—
                              PARATRISSOCLADIUS Zavrel p. 92

35   Costa not, or scarcely, produced beyond R_{4+5}. Anal point well
      developed, usually robust (e.g. fig. 26H)—
                              CHAETOCLADIUS Kieffer p. 82
—   Costa produced well beyond R_{4+5}. Anal point short and sharply
      pointed (fig. 26J)—   TRISSOCLADIUS Kieffer p. 78

36(33) Anal point covered in fine microtrichia (fig. 27A)—
                              ORTHOSMITTIA Goetghebuer p. 90
—   Anal point lacking fine microtrichia, or absent—   37

37   Anal point bearing several long lateral setae (e.g. fig. 27B-C)—
                              ORTHOCLADIUS van der Wulp p. 68
—   Anal point, if present, lacking lateral setae—   38

38   Anal point short, triangular (fig. 27D). Tip of antenna bearing
      several long curved setae (fig. 27E)—
                              SYNORTHOCLADIUS Thienemann p. 76
—   Anal point absent, or if present it is long, though transparent and
      easily overlooked (e.g. fig. 27F). Antennae without curved apical
      setae—   EUKIEFFERIELLA Thienemann p. 64

39(26) Hypopygium with a distinct anal point—   40
—   Anal point minute or absent—   41

40   Anal point robust and bearing lateral setae (fig. 27G). Humeral pits
      often very large and conspicuous (fig. 27I)—
                              RHEOCRICOTOPUS Thienemann p. 76
—   Anal point slender and bare (fig. 27H). Humeral pits minute—
                              MICROCRICOTOPUS Thienemann & Harnisch p. 68

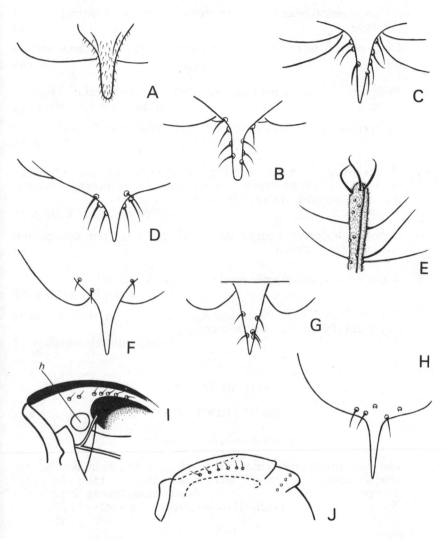

Fig. 27 A-D, anal points of: A, *Orthosmittia albipennis*; B, *Orthocladius (Euorthocladius) rivulorum*; C, *Orthocladius (Orthocladius) rubicundus*; D, *Synorthocladius semivirens*; E, apex of antenna of *S. semivirens*; F-H, anal points of: F, *Eukiefferiella calvescens*; G, *Rheocricotopus effusus*; H, *Microcricotopus rectinervis*; I-J, lateral views of thorax of: I, *Rheocricotopus foveatus* (h = humeral pit); J, *Acricotopus lucens*.

41(39) Dorso-central setae long and upright, arising from distinct pale pits
(fig. 27J)—   **42**

— Dorso-central setae weak and decumbent, not arising from obvious
pits—   **43**

42   Antepronotum unusually large (fig. 28E).   Antennal ratio *c.* 3·0—
ACRICOTOPUS Kieffer p. 54

— Antepronotum normally developed.   Antennal ratio <2·0—
PARATRICHOCLADIUS Santos Abreu p. 74

43(41) Legs usually with pale rings (fig. 28C) and/or abdomen with yellow
markings.   Anterior noto-pleural setae usually absent (fig. 28B) but
if present (fig. 28A) the pale tibial rings are distinct—
CRICOTOPUS van der Wulp p. 56

— Legs and abdomen without pale markings.   Anterior noto-pleural
setae present or absent—   **44**

44   Anterior noto-pleural setae present.   On rocky coasts—
HALOCLADIUS Hirvenoja p. 66

— Anterior noto-pleural setae lacking.   Hypopygium with a minute
anal point (fig. 28D).   Freshwater sp.—
PARACLADIUS Hirvenoja p. 72

KEYS TO SPECIES

Tribe ORTHOCLADIINI

Genus ACRICOTOPUS Kieffer

The only British representative is characterized by its unusually large
antepronotum (fig. 28E) and high antennal ratio (*c.* 3·0).
Hypopygium fig. 96C—   **Acricotopus lucens** (Zetterstedt)
(*Spaniotoma (Trichocladius) lucidus* (Staeg.), Edwards 1929)

Genus BRILLIA Kieffer

1   Outer branch of gonostylus about twice as long as inner branch (fig.
28F).   Hypopygium fig. 97A—   **Brillia longifurca** Kieffer

— The two branches of the gonostylus roughly equal in length (fig.
28G).   Hypopygium fig. 97B—   **B. modesta** (Meigen)

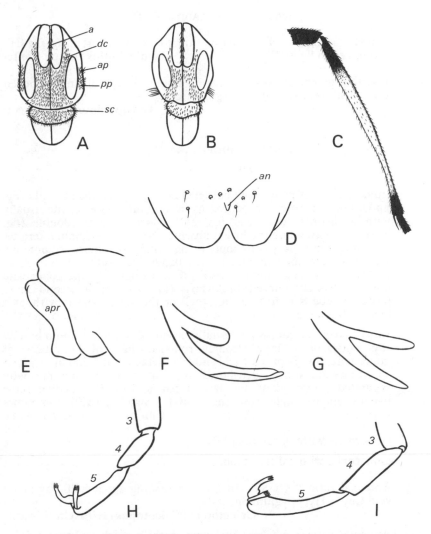

Fig. 28   A-B, dorsal views of thorax of: A, *Cricotopus pilosellus* (*a* = acrostichal setae, *dc* = dorsocentral setae, *ap* = anterior notopleural setae, *pp* = posterior notopleural setae, *sc* = scutellar setae); B, *C. polaris*; C, anterior tibia of *Cricotopus sylvestris*; D, anal tergite of *Paracladius conversus* (*an* = anal point); E, lateral view of anterior part of thorax of *Acricotopus lucens* (*apr* = antepronotum); F-G, gonostyli of: F, *Brillia longifurca*; G, *B. modesta*; H-I, distal tarsal segments of: H, *Cardiocladius fuscus*; I, *C. capucinus*.

Genus CARDIOCLADIUS Kieffer

1 Fourth segment of posterior tarsus very short (fig. 28H). Hypopygium fig. 97C— **Cardiocladius fuscus** Kieffer

— Fourth segment of posterior tarsus longer, though distinctly shorter than fifth (fig. 28I). Hypopygium fig. 97D—
C. capucinus (Zetterstedt)

Genus CRICOTOPUS van der Wulp

(Hirvenoja 1973)

1 Inner margin of gonocoxite flattened or slightly rounded basally (fig. 29A), never distinctly produced as in fig. 29B. Gonocoxite usually with a distinct lobe (e.g. fig. 29I) which may be double (fig. 29H). Occasionally the lobe is absent. Setae on abdominal tergites 3 and 4 uniformly distributed (fig. 29E) or, more commonly, separated into median and lateral bands (fig. 29F); median setae usually in a double row (fig. 29F), if in a single row the gonocoxite lobe is strongly curved backwards (fig. 29I) or a second more posterior lobe is indicated (fig. 30C) or the gonocoxite is without a lobe. Pulvilli lacking— CRICOTOPUS (CRICOTOPUS) **2**

— Inner margin of gonocoxite usually produced to form a hump basally (fig. 29B), or at least strongly rounded (fig. 29C-D). Lobe of gonocoxite always present and single. Setae on abdominal tergite 3 sometimes uniformly distributed over entire surface but normally separated into median and lateral bands, with the median setae usually in a single row (fig. 29G). Small pulvilli sometimes present— CRICOTOPUS (ISOCLADIUS) **16**

2 Gonocoxite without an inner lobe **3**

— Gonocoxite with a distinct lobe **4**

3 Antennal ratio 1·5-1·8. Anal vein extending about half way along vein Cu_2. Hypopygium fig. 98A—
Cricotopus (Cricotopus) trifascia Edwards

— Antennal ratio 1·0-1·3. Anal vein scarcely reaching beyond f.Cu. Hypopygium fig. 98B— **C. (C.) similis** Goetghebuer

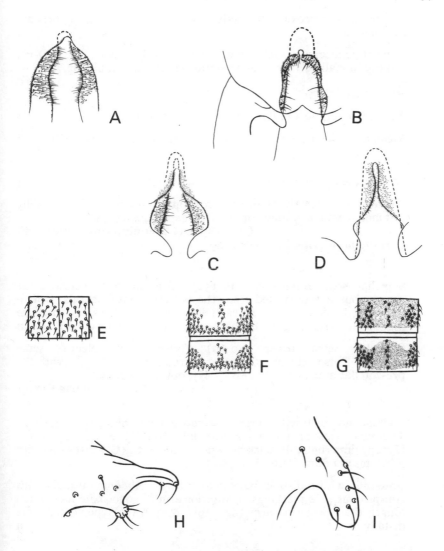

Fig. 29   A-D, ventro-basal area of hypopygium of: A, *Cricotopus (Cricotopus) trifascia*;
B, *C. (Isocladius) sylvestris*; C, *C. (Isocladius) intersectus*; D, *C. (Isocladius)*
brevipalpis; E-G, third and fourth abdominal tergites of: E, *C. (Isocladius)*
reversus; F, *C. (Cricotopus) fuscus*; G, *C. (Isocladius) pilitarsis*; H-I, gonocoxite
lobes of: H, *C. (Cricotopus) triannulatus*; I, *C. (Cricotopus) flavocinctus*.

4(2) Lobe of gonocoxite distinctly double (fig. 30A-B) or broadly
      rectangular—   5

—   Lobe of gonocoxite usually single and relatively slender (fig. 30D-E),
      but occasionally a very small posterior lobe is discernible (fig.
      30C)—
                                                                         10

5   Abdominal tergite 3 uniformly covered with setae   6

—   Median and lateral setae of tergite 3 clearly separated (fig. 29F)— 8

6   At least the anterior tibia with a distinct white ring—   7

—   Tibiae not distinctly ringed. Occasionally slightly paler medially
      but more commonly unicolorous. Hypopygium fig. 98C—
                         Cricotopus (C.) ephippium (Zetterstedt)
      (*Cricotopus lacuum* Edwards 1929)

7   Scutellar setae numerous (130-150). Anterior noto-pleural setae
      present but not separated from the posterior noto-pleurals. Dorso-
      central setae dense (120-180 each side) extending back to scutellum
      (fig. 28A). Hypopygium fig. 98D—   **C. (C.) pilosellus** Brundin

—   Scutellar setae fewer (40-60). Anterior noto-pleural setae
      absent. Dorso-central setae less numerous (*c.* 50 each side) with the
      prescutellar area bare (fig. 28B). Hypopygium fig. 99A—
                                          C. (C.) polaris Kieffer

8(5) Tibiae not distinctly ringed. Abdomen without pale markings.
      The two arms of the gonocoxite lobe roughly equal (fig. 30B).
      Hypopygium (fig. 99B) dark brown—   **C. (C.) fuscus** Kieffer
      (*Cricotopus biformis* Edwards 1929)

—   Fore-tibia with a distinct pale median ring. Abdomen usually with
      conspicuous pale markings. Anterior arm of gonocoxite lobe much
      longer than posterior arm (figs 29H & 30A). Hypopygium pale
      distally—   9

9   Anterior arm of gonocoxite lobe roughly parallel-sided and broadly
      rounded distally (fig. 30A). Hypopygium fig. 99C–
                                  C. (C.) annulator Goetghebuer

—   Anterior arm of gonocoxite lobe tapered, pointed distally (fig.
      29H). Hypopygium fig. 99D—   **C. (C.) triannulatus** (Macquart)

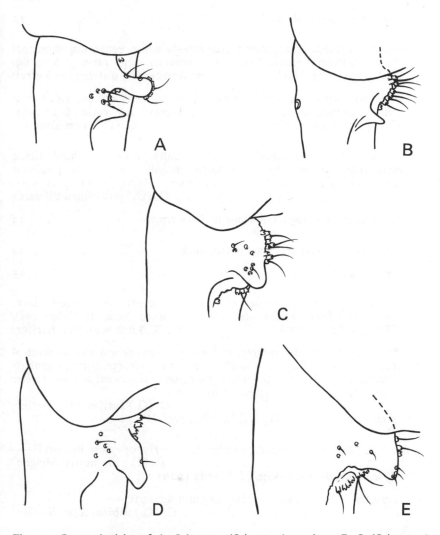

Fig. 30 Gonocoxite lobes of: A, *Cricotopus (Cricotopus) annulator*; B, *C. (Cricotopus) fuscus*; C, *C. (Cricotopus) pulchripes*; D, *C. (Cricotopus) tremulus*; E, *C. (Cricotopus) festivellus*.

10(4) Fore-tarsi partly whitish—   11

—   Fore-tarsi uniformly dark—   12

11   Second segment of anterior tarsus mostly white, remaining segments
     dark. Antennal ratio 1·2-1·4. Anterior leg ratio 0·65-0·69.
     Hypopygium fig. 100A—   **Cricotopus (C.) pulchripes** Verrall

—   Proximal half of segment 3 and whole of segment 2 of anterior tarsus
     white. Antennal ratio 1·4-1·6. Anterior leg ratio 0·57-0·64.
     Hypopygium fig. 100B—   **C. (C.) tremulus** (L.)

12(10) Fore-tibiae indistinctly paler medially. Mid and hind tibiae
     practically unicolorous. Abdomen mainly dark with posterior
     margins of tergites 6 and 7 narrowly pale. Hypopygium fig. 100C—
                                              C. (C.) pallidipes Edwards

—   All tibiae with conspicuous pale median rings—   13

13   Abdominal tergite 4 at least partly dark—   14

—   Tergite 4 yellow—   15

14   Tergite 1 pale, remainder of abdomen mostly or entirely dark.
     Gonocoxite lobe slender and strongly curved backwards (fig. 29I).
     Hypopygium fig. 100D—   **C. (C.) flavocinctus** (Kieffer)

—   At least the posterior quarter of tergite 4 and the anterior quarter of
     tergite 5 pale. Tergites 1 and 2 sometimes pale, remaining segments
     sometimes with pale posterior margins. Gonocoxite lobe rather
     broad (fig. 30E). Hypopygium fig. 101A—
                                           C. (C.) festivellus (Kieffer)
     (*Cricotopus festivus* (Mg.), Edwards 1929)

15(13) Tergites 1 and 4 pale, remainder dark. Hypopygium fig. 101B—
                                             C. (C.) bicinctus (Meigen)
     (*Cricotopus dizonias* (Mg.), Edwards 1929)

—   Tergites 1, 2 and 4 pale. Hypopygium fig. 101C—
                                           C. (C.) albiforceps (Kieffer)

16(1) Inner margin of gonocoxite rounded basally (e.g. fig. 29C-D), not produced— **17**

— Inner margin of gonocoxite produced into a definite hump basally (fig. 29B)— **20**

17 Abdominal tergite 3 uniformly covered with setae. Hypopygium fig. 101D— **C. (Isocladius) reversus** Hirvenoja (*Cricotopus tibialis* (Mg.) Goet., Edwards 1929)

— Median and lateral setae of tergite 3 separated by a bare intermediate area— **18**

18 Maxillary palps very short (fig. 31A), C:P ratio (maximum width of head : length of palp (Fittkau 1962)) 2·1-2·6. Hypopygium fig. 102A— **C. (I.) brevipalpis** Kieffer

— Palps normally developed (fig. 31B), C:P ratio 1·7 or less— **19**

19 Legs and abdomen, including hypopygium, uniformly dark. Hypopygium fig. 102B— **C. (I.) obnixus** (Walker)

— Hypopygium pale distally. Abdominal tergites 1 and 4 sometimes pale. Fore-tibiae sometimes with pale median rings. Hypopygium fig. 102C— **C. (I.) intersectus** (Staeger)

20(16) Abdominal tergite 3 with an incomplete transverse band of setae posteriorly (fig. 31F). Abdomen mainly dark, posterior margin of tergites 6-8 narrowly pale. Tibiae with or without pale median rings. Hypopygium fig. 102 D— **C. (I.) laricomalis** Edwards

— Tergite 3 without a transverse band of setae posteriorly. Abdomen usually distinctly banded. Tibiae always with distinct pale rings— **21**

21 Inner lobe of gonocoxite *c.* 40 μm in breadth, roughly parallel-sided, broadly rounded distally (fig. 31C). Hypopygium fig. 103A— **C. (I.) pilitarsis** (Zetterstedt)

— Gonocoxite lobe much narrower (measured half way along) usually distinctly conical in shape— **22**

22 Beard ratio (length of longest seta : diameter of segment) of third
    segment of anterior tarsus 4·0-6·0.   Fore-tibiae normally dark, mid-
    and hind-tibiae usually with distinct pale rings.   In dark specimens
    only the posterior of tergite 8 is pale, whereas in pale specimens all
    tergites have pale borders.   Hypopygium fig. 103B—
                                            Cricotopus (I.) ornatus (Meigen)

—   Beard ratio only 3·0 or less.   Coloration otherwise—   **23**

23 Pale tibial rings narrow, occupying one third the length of the
    segment which is much more broadly darkened basally than
    distally.   Dorso-central setae numbering between 37 and 43,
    scutellars 26-28.   Abdomen (fig. 31D) with tergite 1 yellow, 4
    darkened at least antero-laterally, 7 pale posteriorly and the
    remainder with more or less distinctly pale margins.   Hypopygium
    fig. 103C—   **C. (I.) speciosus** Goetghebuer

—   Tibial rings broader, occupying about half the segment.   Dorso-
    central setae less than 30, scutellars between 8 and 15—   **24**

24 Tergites 1, 4 and 7 mainly or entirely yellow, remainder dark—   **25**

—   Coloration variable.   Sometimes only the posterior margin of
    tergites 6 and 7 pale, but pale markings may be more extensive.   If
    segments 1, 4 and 7 are predominantly yellow then segment 5 is also
    (e.g. fig. 31E).   Hypopygium fig. 103D—
                                            C. (I.) sylvestris (Fabricius)

25 Prescutellar area of scutum darkened.   Femora dark.   Anterior
    corners of segment 4 sometimes darkened (fig. 31G).   Hypopygium
    fig. 104A—   **C. (I.) tricinctus** (Meigen)

—   Prescutellar area pale.   Femora pale proximally, darkened
    distally.   Any darkening of segment 4 is confined to a central
    triangle (fig. 31H).   Hypopygium fig. 104B—
                                            C. (I.) trifasciatus (Panzer)

N.B.   *Cricotopus (C.) lygropis* Edwards was originally described from the female.   The
male has never been found in the British Isles although Hirvenoja (1973 p. 212) described
a male, tentatively assigned to this species which differs from the known British species in
the possession of a short anal point.

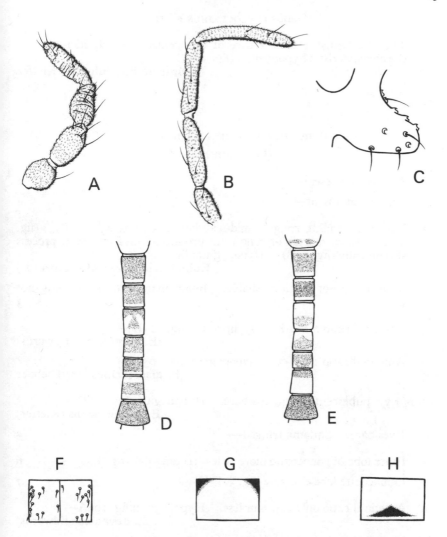

Fig. 31   A-B, maxillary palps of: A, *Cricotopus (Isocladius) brevipalpis*; B, *C. (Cricotopus) fuscus*; C, gonocoxite lobe of *C. (Isocladius) pilitarsis*; D-E, abdominal tergites of: D, *C. (Isocladius) speciosus*; E, *C. (Isocladius) sylvestris*; F, setation of fourth abdominal tergite of *C. (Isocladius) laricomalis*; G-H, fourth abdominal tergites of: G, *C. (Isocladius) tricinctus*; H, *C. (Isocladius) trifasciatus*.

Genus DIPLOCLADIUS Kieffer

The sole British representative of this genus is readily identified by the characteristic hypopygium (fig. 104C)—
Diplocladius cultriger Kieffer

Genus EUKIEFFERIELLA Thienemann
(Lehmann 1972)

1   Anal point present—   2

—   Anal point absent—   4

2   Vein R_{2+3} ending roughly mid-way between veins R_1 and R_{4+5} (fig. 32A). Inner margin of gonostylus produced into a tooth-like process sub-apically (fig. 32B). Hypopygium fig. 105A—
Eukiefferiella verralli (Edwards)

—   Vein R_{2+3} not distinguishable. Inner margin of gonostylus not produced—   3

3   Antennal ratio 0·6-0·8. Hypopygium fig. 105B—
E. calvescens (Edwards)

—   Antennal ratio 1·0-1·3. Hypopygium fig. 105C—
E. discoloripes Goetghebuer

4(1) Eyes pubescent. Squama bare. Hypopygium fig. 105D—
E. coerulescens (Kieffer)

—   Eyes bare. Squama fringed—   5

5   Inner lobe of gonocoxite more or less rectangular (fig. 32C)—   6

—   Gonocoxite lobe elongate (fig. 32F-H)—   7

6   Antennal ratio only c. 0·6 or less. Hypopygium fig. 106A—
E. devonica (Edwards)

—   Antennal ratio c. 0·9. Hypopygium fig. 106B—
E. ilkleyensis (Edwards)

7(5) Gonostylus of unusual shape, strongly expanded proximally (fig. 32D). Hypopygium fig. 106C—   **E. gracei** (Edwards)
(*E. potthasti* Lehmann 1972)

—   Gonostylus not expanded proximally—   8

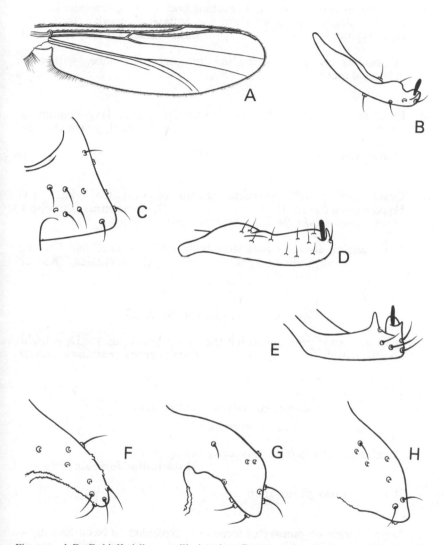

Fig. 32 A-B, *Eukiefferiella verralli*: A, wing; B, gonostylus; C, gonocoxite lobe of *E. ilkleyensis*; D-E, gonostyli of: D, *E. gracei*; E, *E. minor*; F-H, gonocoxite lobes of: F, *E. clypeata*; G, *E. claripennis*; H, *E. brevicalcar*.

8 Gonostylus rather short, not reaching back to the gonocoxite lobe, its inner margin produced into a subapical tooth (fig. 32E). Hypopygium fig. 106D— **Eukiefferiella minor** (Edwards)

— Gonostylus elongate, extending to gonocoxite lobe, without a subapical tooth— **9**

9 Inner lobe of gonocoxite very slender (fig. 32F). Hypopygium fig. 107A— **E. clypeata** (Kieffer)

— Gonocoxite lobe broader (fig. 32G-H)— **10**

10 Costa ending well proximal to tip of vein Cu_1 (fig. 33A). Hypopygium fig. 107B— **E. claripennis** (Lundbeck) (*Spaniotoma (Eukiefferiella) hospita* Edwards 1929)

— Costa ending above or only slightly proximal to tip of vein Cu_1 (fig. 33B). Hypopygium fig. 107C— **E. brevicalcar** (Kieffer)

Genus EURYCNEMUS van der Wulp

A monospecific genus in which the hypopygium (fig. 107D) is highly characteristic— **Eurycnemus crassipes** (Panzer)

Genus HALOCLADIUS Hirvenoja
(Hirvenoja 1973)

1 Antennal ratio 0·6-0·7. Hypopygium fig. 108A— **Halocladius fucicola** (Edwards)

— Antennal ratio greater than 1·0— **2**

2 Inner margin of gonostylus somewhat expanded on basal half to two thirds (fig. 33C). Hypopygium fig. 108B— **H. variabilis** (Staeger)

— Gonostylus narrow basally (fig. 33D). Hypopygium fig. 108C— **H. varians** (Staeger) (*Cricotopus vitripennis* (Meigen)) (*Cricotopus vitripennis* var. *halophilus* (Kieffer))

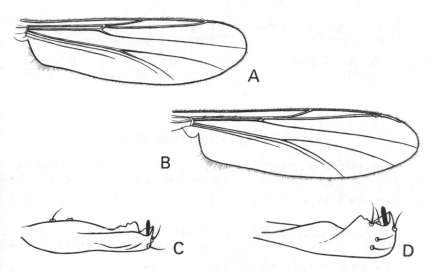

Fig. 33 A-B, wings of: A, *Eukiefferiella claripennis*; B, *E. brevicalcar*; C-D, gonostyli of: C, *Halocladius variabilis*; D, *H. varians*.

Genus HETEROTANYTARSUS Sparck

There is only one representative of this genus known from the British Isles. The hypopygium (fig. 108D) is very characteristic—

Heterotanytarsus apicalis (Kieffer)

Genus HETEROTRISSOCLADIUS Sparck

1 Smaller species (wing length *c.* 2·5 mm). Wing membrane with macrotrichia near tip only. Hypopygium fig. 109A—

Heterotrissocladius grimshawi (Edwards)

— Larger species (wing length 3·5-4·0 mm). Wing membrane with macrotrichia over entire surface. Hypopygium fig. 109B—

H. marcidus (Walker)

Genus MICROCRICOTOPUS Thienemann & Harnisch
(Fittkau & Lehmann 1970)

1 Inner lobe of gonocoxite roughly rectangular (fig. 34A).
Hypopygium fig. 109C— **Microcricotopus bicolor** (Zetterstedt)

— Inner lobe of gonocoxite conical in shape (fig. 34B). Hypopygium
fig. 109D— **M. rectinervis** (Kieffer)

Genus ORTHOCLADIUS van der Wulp

1 Inner margin of gonocoxite produced into two separate lobes (fig.
34C-E)— ORTHOCLADIUS (EUDACTYLOCLADIUS) 4

— Gonocoxite not as above— 2

2 Anal point rounded distally (e.g. fig. 34F)—
ORTHOCLADIUS (EUORTHOCLADIUS) 6

— Anal point tapered to a point (e.g. fig. 34G)— 3

3 Anal point long (fig. 34G). Lobe of gonocoxite slender, finger-like
(fig. 34H). Antennal ratio 2·2-2·5. Anal lobe of wing strongly
produced (fig. 35A). Fore-tarsus with long beard. Hypopygium
fig. 110A—
Orthocladius (Pogonocladius) consobrinus (Holmgren)

— Without the above combination of characters—
ORTHOCLADIUS (ORTHOCLADIUS) 8

4(1) Anal point robust (fig. 35B). The lobes of the gonocoxite adjacent
as in fig. 34C. Hypopygium fig. 110B—
Orthocladius (Eudactylocladius) gelidus Kieffer
(*Hydrobaenus (Orthocladius) grampianus* Edwards, Coe 1950)

— Anal point slender (fig. 35C-D). Gonocoxite lobes well separated
(fig. 34D-E).— 5

5 Anterior lobe of gonocoxite right-angled, posterior lobe slightly
developed (fig. 34D). Hypopygium fig. 110C—
O. (E.) obtexens Brundin

— Anterior lobe more rounded, posterior lobe prominent (fig. 34E).
Hypopygium fig. 110D— **Orthocladius (Eudactylocladius) sp. a**

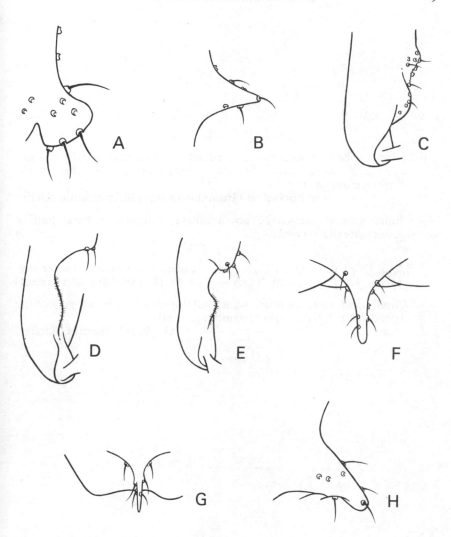

Fig. 34   A-B, gonocoxite lobes of: A, *Microcricotopus bicolor*; B, *M. rectinervis*; C-E, gonocoxites of: C, *Orthocladius (Eudactylocladius) gelidus*; D, *O. (Eudactylocladius) obtexens*; E, *Orthocladius (Eudactylocladius)* sp.a; F-G, anal points of: F, *O. (Euorthocladius) rivulorum*; G, *O. (Pogonocladius) consobrinus*; H, gonocoxite lobe of *O. (Pogonocladius) consobrinus*.

6(2) Inner lobe of gonocoxite very broad and characteristically shaped,
extending more than halfway along gonocoxite (fig. 35E).
Hypopygium fig. 111C—
                    Orthocladius (Euorthocladius) thienemanni Kieffer

—   Inner lobe of gonocoxite not as above, confined to basal half of
gonocoxite (fig. 35F-G)—   **7**

7   Anal point very broad (fig. 35H).   Lobe of gonocoxite slender (fig.
35F).   Hypopygium fig. 111A—   **O. (E.) frigidus** (Zetterstedt)

—   Anal point more slender, somewhat tapered.   Lobe of gonocoxite
broader (fig. 35G).   Hypopygium fig. 111B—
                                      O. (E.) rivulorum (Kieffer)

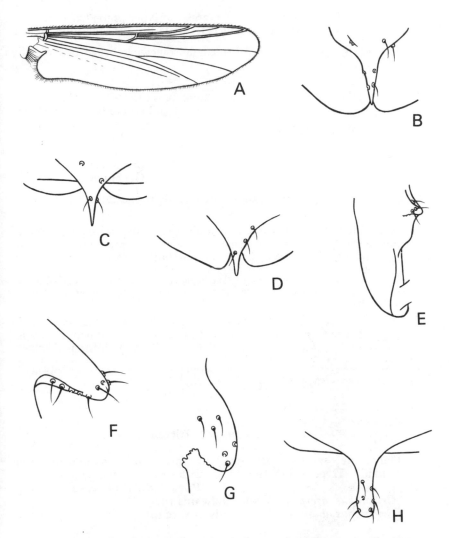

Fig. 35   A, wing of *Orthocladius (Pogonocladius) consobrinus*; B-D, anal points of: B, *O. (Eudactylocladius) gelidus*; C, *O. (Eudactylocladius) obtexens*; D, *O. (Eudactylocladius)* sp.a; E, gonocoxite of *Orthocladius (Euorthocladius) thienemanni*; F-G, gonocoxite lobes of F, *O. (Euorthocladius) frigidus*; G, *O. (Euorthocladius) rivulorum*; H, anal point of *O. (Euorthocladius) frigidus.*

8(3) Gonostylus tapered distally (fig. 36A). Hypopygium fig. 112A—
      Orthocladius (Orthocladius) rubicundus Meigen

—   Gonostylus roughly parallel-sided or somewhat broadened distally
      (fig. 36B)—   9

9   Antennal ratio 2·5-3·0. Hypopygium fig. 112B—
                                    O. (O.) glabripennis (Goetghebuer)

—   Antennal ratio <2·4   10

10   Gonocoxite produced ventro-basally into a short, finger-like lobe (fig.
      36C). Hypopygium fig. 112C—   **O. (O.) rhyacobius** Kieffer

—   Ventro-basal contour of gonocoxite broadly rounded (fig. 38D)—   11

11   Anal point long, drawn out distally (fig. 36E). Last segment of
      maxillary palp 1·7-1·8 times as long as preceding segment.
      Hypopygium fig. 113A—   **Orthocladius (Orthocladius) sp. a**

The identity of this species is uncertain. The hypopygium resembles that figured for *O.*
oblidens by Brundin (1947) but examination of Walker's type of *O. oblidens* has shown it
to be another species.

—   Anal point more broadly triangular (fig. 36F). Last segment of palp
      1·3-1·4 times as long as preceding segment. Hypopygium fig.
      113B—   **O. (O.) oblidens** (Walker)

Since there is some confusion over the true identity of *O. oblidens* the hypopygium is
drawn from Walker's type on which the anal point is slightly twisted.

Genus PARACLADIUS Hirvenoja

Only one species belonging to this genus is known from
Britain. Hypopygium (fig. 113C) with a minute anal point—
                                    Paracladius conversus (Walker)
(*Cricotopus inserpens* (Walk.), Edwards 1929)
(*Cricotopus obtexens* (Walk.), Edwards 1929)

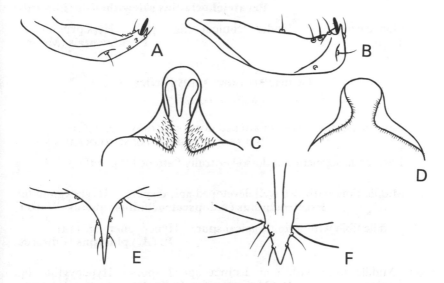

Fig. 36 A-B, gonostyli of: A, *Orthocladius (Orthocladius) rubicundus*; B, *O.*
(Orthocladius) glabripennis; C-D, ventro-basal contour of gonocoxite of: C, *O.*
(Orthocladius) rhyacobius; D, *O. (Orthocladius) oblidens*; E-F, anal points of: E,
Orthocladius (Orthocladius) sp.a; F, *O. (Orthocladius) oblidens*.

Genus PARATRICHOCLADIUS Santos Abreu

1   Gonocoxite lobe broad (fig. 37A).   Hypopygium fig. 114A—
Paratrichocladius skirwithensis (Edwards)

—   Gonocoxite lobe slender, conical (fig. 37B).   Hypopygium fig.
114B—   P. rufiventris (Meigen)

Genus PSECTROCLADIUS Kieffer
(Wülker 1956)

1   Last segment of all tarsi flattened dorso-ventrally (fig. 37C)—
PSECTROCLADIUS (ALLOPSECTROCLADIUS)— 2

—   Last tarsal segment not dorso-ventrally flattened (fig. 37D)—   3

2   Middle tibia with two well developed apical spurs.   Hypopygium fig.
114C—   Psectrocladius (Allopsectrocladius) obvius (Walker)

—   Middle tibia with a single apical spur.   Hypopygium fig. 114D—
P. (A.) platypus (Edwards)

3(1) Middle tibia with two distinct apical spurs.   Hypopygium fig.
115A—   P. (Monopsectrocladius) calcaratus (Edwards)

—   Middle tibia with a single apical spur—   PSECTROCLADIUS s. s.— 4

4   Anal tergite triangular, without a distinct anal point (fig. 37E).
Hypopygium fig. 115B—   P. turfaceus Kieffer

—   Anal tergite with a distinct anal point (e.g. fig. 37F-I)—   5

5   Anal tergite rounded, anal point peg-like (fig. 37F).   Hypopygium
fig. 115C—   P. psilopterus Kieffer

—   Anal tergite more or less triangular, (fig. 37G-I)—   6

6   Anal point long, uniformly tapered from base to tip (fig. 37I).
Hypopygium fig. 116B–   P. sordidellus (Zetterstedt)

—   Anal point rather abruptly broadened basally (fig. 37G-H)—   7

7   Anterior tarsus with a long beard.   Antennal ratio >2.
Hypopygium fig. 116A—   P. barbimanus (Edwards)

—   Anterior tarsus without a beard.   Antennal ratio <2—   8

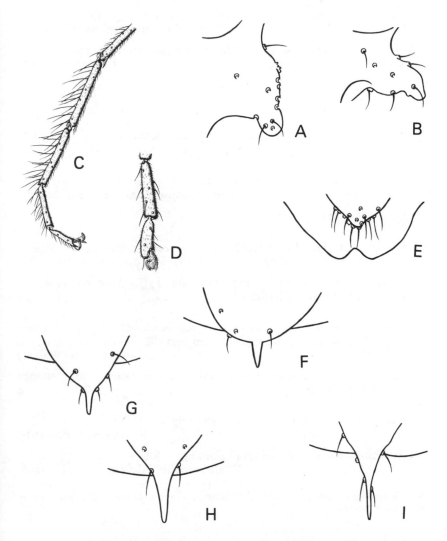

Fig. 37 A-B, gonocoxite lobes of: A, *Paratrichocladius skirwithensis*; B, *P. rufiventris*; C-D, apical segments of anterior tarsi of: C, *Psectrocladius (Allopsectrocladius) obvius* (last segment dorso-ventrally compressed); D, *P. (Psectrocladius) sordidellus* (last segment cylindrical); E-I, anal points of: E, *P. (Psectrocladius) turfaceus*; F, *P. (Psectrocladius) psilopterus*; G, *P. (Psectrocladius) barbimanus*; H, *P. (Psectrocladius) limbatellus*; I, *P. (Psectrocladius) sordidellus*.

8 Gonocoxite lobe rectangular, posterior margin straight (fig. 38A). Hypopygium fig. 116C— **Psectrocladius limbatellus** (Holmgren)

— Gonocoxite lobe rounded, posterior margin strongly produced (fig. 38B). Hypopygium fig. 116D— **P. fennicus** Storå

Genus RHEOCRICOTOPUS Thienemann
(Lehmann 1969)

1 Gonostylus curved sharply upwards at tip (fig. 38C). Hypopygium fig. 117A— **Rheocricotopus chalybeatus** (Edwards)

— Gonostylus not as above 2

2 Humeral pits small and indistinct. Gonostylus lacking a preapical tooth (fig. 38D). Hypopygium fig. 117B— **R. dispar** (Goetghebuer)

— Humeral pits large and conspicuous (fig. 27I). Gonostylus with a distinct preapical tooth (fig. 38E-G)— 3

3 Preapical tooth of gonostylus low and broad (fig. 38E). Median angle of gonocoxite lobe slightly produced (fig. 38H). Hypopygium fig. 117C— **R. effusus** (Walker)

— Preapical tooth narrower (fig. 38F-G). Gonocoxite lobe shaped differently (fig. 38I-J)— 4

4 Antennal ratio 1·0-1·1. Hypopygium fig. 117D—
R. foveatus (Edwards)

— Antennal ratio *c.* 1·7. Hypopygium fig. 118A—
R. glabricollis (Meigen) sensu Edwards

N.B. According to Lehmann (1969) this species is a nomen nudum. It is used here in Edwards's (1929) sense.

Genus SYNORTHOCLADIUS Thienemann

Only one species is known from the British Isles. The hypopygium is distinctive (fig. 118B)— **Synorthocladius semivirens** (Kieffer)
(Spaniotoma (Orthocladius) tripilata Edwards 1929)

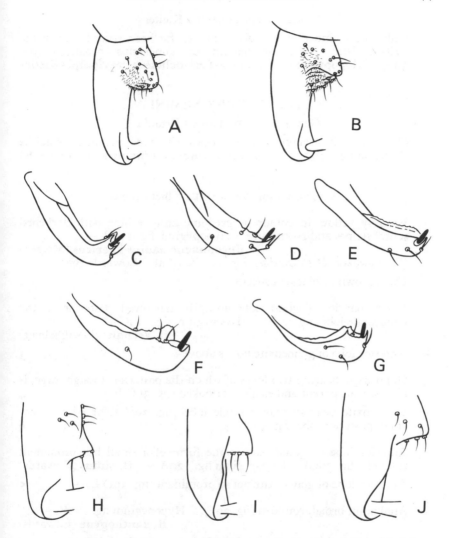

Fig. 38   A-B, gonocoxite lobes of: A, *Psectrocladius (Psectrocladius) limbatellus*; B, *P. (Psectrocladius) fennicus*; C-G, gonostyli of: C, *Rheocricotopus chalybeatus*; D, *R. dispar*; E, *R. effusus*; F, *R. foveatus*; G, *R. glabricollis*; H-J, gonocoxites of: H, *R. effusus*; I, *R. foveatus*; J, *R. glabricollis*.

Genus TRISSOCLADIUS Kieffer

Only one member of this genus has so far been recorded from the British Isles. Posterior margin of gonostylus produced (fig. 39A). Hypopygium fig. 118C— **Trissocladius brevipalpis** Kieffer

Tribe METRIOCNEMINI

Genus ACAMPTOCLADIUS Brundin

Contains only a single British species, the hypopygium of which is shown in fig. 119A— **Acamptocladius submontanus** (Edwards)

Genus BRYOPHAENOCLADIUS Thienemann

1 Entirely yellow in colour or predominantly yellow with darkened scutal stripes and postnotum. Hypopygium fig. 119B—
Bryophaenocladius ictericus (Meigen)
(*Spaniotoma (Orthocladius) bipunctella* (Zett.), Edwards 1929)

— Dark brown or blackish species— 2

2 Inner margin of gonocoxite abruptly narrowed posterior to the gonocoxite lobe (fig. 39B). Hypopygium fig. 119C—
B. vernalis (Goetghebuer)

— Anterior lobe of gonocoxite not as above— 3

3 Gonocoxite bearing two lobes of which the posterior, though large, is almost transparent and easily overlooked (fig. 39C-E)— 4

— Gonocoxite bearing only a single lobe (fig. 39H-J) or with a very small posterior lobe (fig. 40A)— 6

4 Anterior lobe of gonocoxite in the form of a small but prominent tubercle (fig. 39C). Hypopygium fig. 120A— **B. simus** (Edwards)

— Anterior lobe of gonocoxite not so prominent (fig. 39D-E)— 5

5 Anal point broad, rounded (fig. 39F). Hypopygium fig. 120B—
B. xanthogyne (Edwards)

— Anal point triangular (fig. 39G). Hypopygium fig. 120C—
Bryophaenocladius sp. cf. **scanicus** (Brundin)
(*Orthocladius (Eudactylocladius) scanicus* Brundin 1947, Kloet & Hincks 1975)

N.B. This species is represented in the British Museum (Natural History) collection by a single specimen which differs from Brundin's (1947) figure of *B. scanicus* in the shape of the anal point.

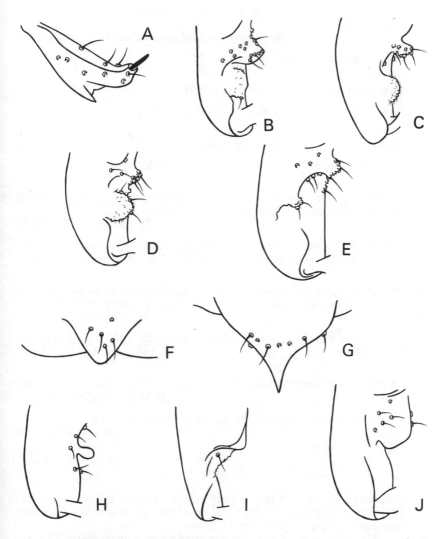

Fig. 39 A, gonostylus of *Trissocladius brevipalpis*; B-E, gonocoxites of: B, *Bryophaenocladius vernalis*; C, *B. simus*; D, *B. xanthogyne*; E, *B.* cf. *scanicus*; F-G, anal points of: F, *B. xanthogyne*; G, *B.* cf. *scanicus*; H-J, gonocoxites of: H, *B. nitidicollis*; I, *B. femineus*; J, *B. illimbatus*.

6(3) Lobe of gonocoxite in the form of a small bare papilla (fig. 39H). Hypopygium fig. 121A—
$\qquad$ **Bryophaenocladius nitidicollis** (Goetghebuer)

— Lobe of gonocoxite not as above—   7

7   Anal point broadly rounded (fig. 40E-H)—   **8**

— Anal point long and relatively slender (fig. 40I-J)—   **11**

8   Gonocoxite lobe very large (fig. 39I-J)—   **9**

— Gonocoxite lobe in the form of a small tubercle (fig. 40A-B)—   **10**

9   Gonocoxite lobe squarish (fig. 39I).   Outer margin of gonostylus smoothly rounded.   Hypopygium fig. 121B—
$\qquad$ **B. femineus** (Edwards)

— Gonocoxite lobe rounded (fig. 39J).   Gonostylus abruptly bent inwards at tip.   Hypopygium fig. 121C—   **B. illimbatus** (Edwards)

10(8) In addition to the small anterior lobe, the gonocoxite also bears a very small posterior lobe (fig. 40A).   Hypopygium fig. 121D—
$\qquad$ **B. nidorum** (Edwards)

— Gonocoxite with no trace of a second lobe (fig. 40B).   Hypopygium fig. 122A—   **B. tuberculatus** (Edwards)

11(7) Lobe of gonocoxite bent apically (fig. 40C).   Hypopygium fig. 122B—   **B. subvernalis** (Edwards)

— Lobe of gonocoxite conical (fig. 40D).   Hypopygium fig. 122C—
$\qquad$ **B. aestivus** Brundin

Genus CAMPTOCLADIUS van der Wulp

Contains only one British species.   The antenna bears broad leaf-like setae on the second, third and terminal segments of the flagellum (fig. 40K).   Hypopygium fig. 122D—
$\qquad$ **Camptocladius stercorarius** (Degeer)

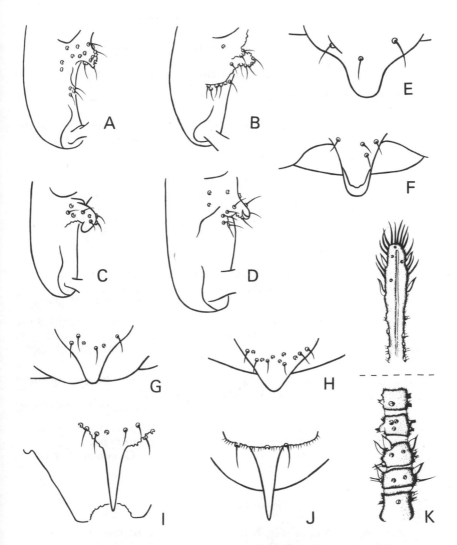

Fig. 40   A-D, gonocoxites of: A, *Bryophaenocladius nidorum*; B, *B. tuberculatus*; C, *B. subvernalis*; D, *B. aestivus*; E-J, anal points of: E, *B. femineus*; F, *B. illimbatus*; G, *B. nidorum*; H, *B. tuberculatus*; I, *B. subvernalis*; J, *B. aestivus*; K, basal segments and apex of antennal flagellum of *Camptocladius stercorarius*.

Genus CHAETOCLADIUS Kieffer

1　Outer margin of gonostylus produced into a distinct 'tooth' (fig. 41A).　Hypopygium fig. 123A—
Chaetocladius dentiforceps (Edwards)

—　Gonostylus not as above—　　　　　　　　　　　　　　　**2**

2　Anal point very slender and delicate in appearance (fig. 41B). Hypopygium fig. 123B—　　　　　　**C. dissipatus** (Edwards)

—　Anal point otherwise—　　　　　　　　　　　　　　　**3**

3　Anal point short reaching only about halfway along the gonocoxite lobe (fig. 41C-D)—　　　　　　　　　　　　　　　　　　　**4**

—　Anal point extending to tip of gonocoxite lobe or beyond (fig. 41G-H)—　　　　　　　　　　　　　　　　　　　　　　　　**5**

4　Gonocoxite lobe large, occupying about three-quarters of the inner margin of the gonocoxite (fig. 41E).　Hypopygium fig. 123C—
C. perennis (Meigen)

—　Gonocoxite lobe occupying only about half of the inner margin of the gonocoxite and differently shaped (fig. 41F).　Hypopygium fig. 123D—　　　　　　　　　　　　　　　　**C. melaleucus** (Meigen)

5(3) Anal point triangular (fig. 41G) and extending well beyond the inner lobe of the gonocoxite.　Hypopygium fig. 124A—
C. piger (Goetghebuer)

—　Anal point roughly parallel-sided and distally rounded (fig. 41H), not reaching beyond the gonocoxite lobe.　Hypopygium fig. 124B—
C. suecicus (Kieffer)

Genus CLUNIO Haliday

A marine genus of which there is only one British representative. The hypopygium (fig. 124C) is distinctive—
Clunio marinus Haliday

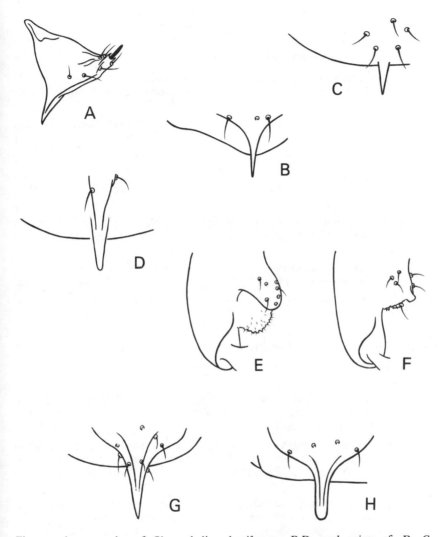

Fig. 41 A, gonostylus of *Chaetocladius dentiforceps*; B-D, anal points of: B, *C. dissipatus*; C, *C. melaleucus*; D, *C. perennis*; E-F, gonocoxites of: E, *C. perennis*; F, *C. melaleucus*; G-H, anal points of: G, *C. piger*; H, *C. suecicus*.

Genus CORYNONEURA Winnertz
(Schlee 1968)

1 Tip of antenna with a group of setae (e.g. fig. 42A)—   **2**

— Tip of antenna bare (fig. 42B). Hypopygium fig. 124D—
Corynoneura carriana Edwards

2 Gonocoxite without an inner lobe, or with only a very slight lobe (fig. 42C-D)—   **3**

— Gonocoxite with a prominent lobe (fig. 42G-J)—   **5**

3 Last antennal segment as long as preceding 6-8 segments combined—   **4**

— Last antennal segment only as long as preceding 2 or 3 segments combined. Hypopygium fig. 125C—   **C. celtica** Edwards

4 Gonostylus strongly curved and tapered to a finely-pointed apex (fig. 42E). Hypopygium fig. 125B—   **C. edwardsi** Brundin

— Gonostylus as in fig. 42F; not tapered distally. Hypopygium fig. 125A—   **C. scutellata** Winnertz

5(2) Antennal filament 12-segmented—   **6**

— Antennal filament 10- or 11-segmented—   **7**

6 Last antennal segment as long as the preceding 8 segments combined. Inner lobe extending more than halfway along gonocoxite (fig. 42G). Hypopygium fig. 125D—   **C. celeripes** Winnertz

— Last antennal segment only as long as preceding 4 segments combined. Inner lobe extending almost to tip of gonocoxite (fig. 42H). Hypopygium fig. 126A—   **C. lacustris** Edwards

7(5) Antennal filament comprising 11 segments. Last segment as long as preceding 8 combined. Gonocoxite lobe rounded (fig. 42I). Hypopygium fig. 126B—   **C. coronata** Edwards

— Antennal filament comprising 10 segments. Last segment equal in length to preceding 4-6 combined. Gonocoxite lobe as in fig. 42J. Hypopygium fig. 126C—   **C. lobata** Edwards

One other species, *C. fuscihalter* Edwards, is known from the female only. It differs from all other British species of the genus in having darkened halteres.

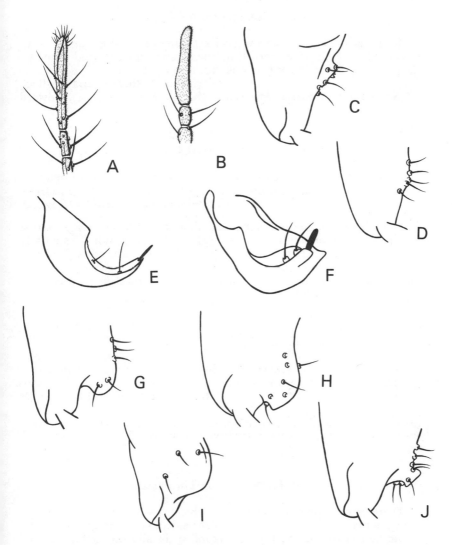

Fig. 42   A-B, apices of antennal flagellum of: A, *Corynoneura celtica*; B, *C. carriana*; C-
D, gonocoxites of: C, *C. celtica*; D, *C. scutellata*; E-F, gonostyli of: E, *C.
edwardsi*; F, *C. scutellata*; G-J, gonocoxites of: G, *C. celeripes*; H, *C. lacustris*; I,
C. coronata; J, *C. lobata*.

Genus EPOICOCLADIUS Zavrel

There is only one British species belonging to this genus, which should be readily identified from the characters mentioned in the key to genera. The hypopygium is shown in fig. 126D—

Epoicocladius flavens (Malloch)
(*Spaniotoma (Smittia) ephemerae* (Kieff., in Zavrel 1924), Edwards 1929)

Genus GYMNOMETRIOCNEMUS Goetghebuer

1 Dark species, thorax black with scutal stripes fused.   Inner margin of gonostylus expanded medially (fig. 43A).   Hypopygium fig. 127A—
Gymnometriocnemus brumalis (Edwards)

— Paler species, ground colour of thorax yellowish, scutal stripes separate.   Gonostylus   (fig.   43B)   not   expanded   medially. Hypopygium fig. 127B—   **G. subnudus** (Edwards)

A third species, *G. brevitarsis* Edwards is known only from the female and is characterized by a very low leg ratio of about 0·35.

Genus HELENIELLA Gowin

Only one species is known from Britain and is easily identified from the characters given in the key to genera and from the distinctive hypopygium (fig. 127C)—   **Heleniella ornaticollis** (Edwards)

A specimen from Dorset differs from the type material in having a small anal point and a strongly produced posterior margin to the lobe of the gonocoxite (fig. 127D).

Genus KRENOSMITTIA Thienemann

There is only one British species which is very small (wing length *c.* 1·2 mm) and has a very low antennal ratio (*c.* 0·35).   The lobe of the gonocoxite of the type is expanded distally (fig. 43C) although Edwards's figure does not show this.   The hypopygium is shown in fig. 128A—   **Krenosmittia camptophleps** (Edwards)

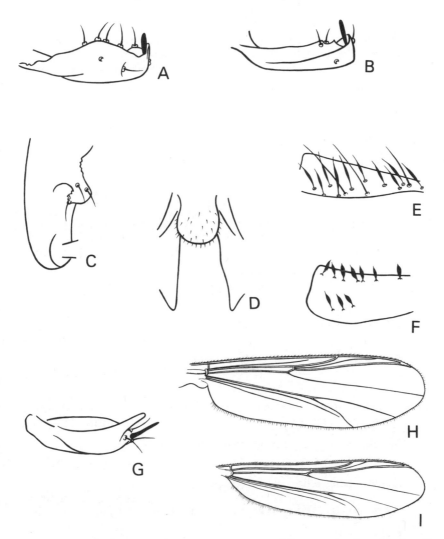

Fig. 43   A-B, gonostyli of: A, *Gymnometriocnemus brumalis*; B, *G. subnudus*; C, gonocoxite of *Krenosmittia camptophleps*; D, globular ventro-basal appendage of hypopygium of *Limnophyes* sp. nr *globifer*; E-F, prescutellar setae of: E, *L. prolongatus*; F, *L. truncorum*; G, gonostylus of *L. truncorum*; H-I, wings of: H, *L. habilis*; I, *L. minimus*.

Genus LIMNOPHYES Eaton

I   Hypopygium with a large globose appendage ventrally between the bases of the gonocoxites (fig. 43D). Hypopygium fig. 128B—
                                      Limnophyes sp. nr **globifer** Brundin

—   Hypopygium not as above—   **2**

2   Numerous lamellar setae present on the prescutellar area of the scutum (fig. 43E-F)—   **3**

—   Prescutellar area with simple setae only or with very few scattered lamellar setae—   **5**

3   Gonostylus with a long, slender subapical spine (fig. 43G). Lamellar setae (fig. 43F) relatively short (*c.* 22 μm) and broad (5-6 μm), easily overlooked at low magnifications. Hypopygium fig. 128C—
                                      L. truncorum (Goetghebuer)

—   Gonostylus without a subapical spine. Lamellar setae (fig. 43E) long (43-51 μm) and slender (3-4 μm)—   **4**

4   Antennal ratio 0·3 or less. Hypopygium fig. 128D—
                                      L. gurgicola (Edwards)

—   Antennal ratio 0·5-0·6. Hypopygium fig. 129A—
                                  L. prolongatus (Kieffer)

5(2)   Scutum with a dense field of lamellar setae on shoulders. Hypopygium fig. 129B—   **L. pumilio** (Holmgren)

—   Shoulders with very few or no lamellar setae—   **6**

6   Halteres pale, yellowish. Hypopygium fig. 129C—
                                  L. exiguus (Goetghebuer)
(*Spaniotoma (Limnophyes) pusilla* Eat., Edwards 1929)

—   Halteres dark—   **7**

7   Anal lobe of wing well developed, right-angled (fig. 43H). Hypopygium fig. 129D—   **L. habilis** (Walker)

—   Anal lobe obtuse (fig. 43I). Hypopygium fig. 130A—
                                  L. minimus (Meigen)

Genus MESOSMITTIA Brundin

Only one species is known from the British Isles. Hypopygium as in fig. 130B— **Mesosmittia flexuella** (Edwards)

Genus METRIOCNEMUS van der Wulp

1   Entire wing membrane rather densely clothed with macrotrichia— **2**

—   Basal half of wing bare or with a few scattered macrotrichia, apical half more densely covered— **9**

2   Gonocoxite with a pronounced lobe on basal half (fig. 44A-B)— **3**

—   Gonocoxite lobe less pronounced (fig. 44C)— **5**

3   Antennal ratio about 1·0.   Hypopygium fig. 130C— **Metriocnemus cavicola** Kieffer (*M. martinii* Tnm., Edwards 1929)

—   Antennal ratio at least 1·5— **4**

4   Halteres blackened.   Hypopygium fig. 130D— **M. hygropetricus** (Kieffer) (*M. longitarsus*, Goet., Edwards 1929)

—   Halteres pale.   Hypopygium (fig. 131A) similar to above species— **M. hirticollis** (Staeger)

N.B.   These two species as interpreted by Edwards are very similar and may not be distinct.

5(2) Antennal ratio 2·5-3·0.   Hypopygium fig. 131B—
M. picipes (Meigen)

— Antennal ratio 2·0 or less—   **6**

6   Anal point long (fig. 44D).   Antennal ratio only about 0·5.
Hypopygium fig. 131C—   **M. gracei** Edwards

— Anal point short (fig. 44E-G).   Antennal ratio about 1·0 or more—**7**

7   Antennal ratio only about 1·0-1·2—   **8**

— Antennal ratio approaching 2·0.   Hypopygium fig. 131D—
M. atriclavus Kieffer

8   First segment of posterior tarsus about one third as long as
tibia.   Hypopygium fig. 132A—   **M. fuscipes** (Meigen)

— First segment of posterior tarsus about half as long as
tibia.   Hypopygium fig. 132B—   **M. atratulus** (Zetterstedt)

9(1) Anal point rather slender, tapering to a point distally (fig. 44H).
Basal half of wing membrane with a few macrotrichia
posteriorly.   Hypopygium fig. 132C—   **M. tristellus** Edwards

— Anal point more robust, bluntly rounded distally (fig. 44I).
Basal half of wing membrane bare.   Hypopygium fig. 132D—
M. ursinus (Holmgren)

Genus ORTHOSMITTIA Goetghebuer

1   Lobe of gonocoxite large, rounded and bearing several long setae (fig.
45A).   Occurs on rocky coasts.   Hypopygium fig. 133A—
Orthosmittia brevifurcata (Edwards)

— Gonocoxite lobe smaller, slender and bare (fig. 45B).   Hypopygium
fig. 133B—   **O. albipennis** (Goetghebuer)

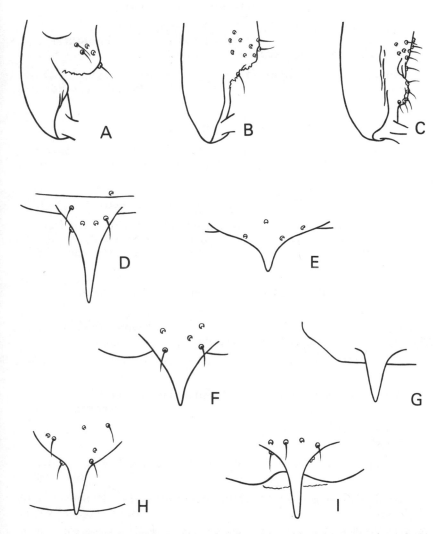

Fig. 44   A-C, gonocoxites of: A, *Metriocnemus cavicola*; B, *M. hygropetricus*; C, *M. picipes*; D-I, anal points of: D, *M. gracei*; E, *M. atriclavus*; F, *M. fuscipes*; G, *M. atratulus*; H, *M. tristellus*; I, *M. ursinus*.

Genus PARAKIEFFERIELLA Thienemann

1   Anal point triangular (fig. 45C).   Hypopygium fig. 133C—
                     Parakiefferiella bathophila (Kieffer)
    (*Spaniotoma (Smittia) cheethami* Edwards 1929)

—   Anal point broadly rounded (fig. 45D).   Hypopygium fig. 133D—
                                   P. coronata (Edwards)

Genus PARALIMNOPHYES Brundin

Only one species is known from the British Isles.   Hypopygium fig.
134A—   **Paralimnophyes hydrophilus** (Goetghebuer)

Genus PARAMETRIOCNEMUS Goetghebuer

Only one representative of this genus has been recorded from the
British Isles, the hypopygium of which is illustrated in fig. 134B—
                     Parametriocnemus stylatus (Kieffer)

Genus PARAPHAENOCLADIUS Sparck & Thienemann

1   Anal point very slender, pointed distally (fig. 45E).   Hypopygium
    fig. 134C—   **Paraphaenocladius sp. a**
    This is known from a single specimen taken from a small seepage in Dorset.

—   Anal point broader distally, rounded at tip (fig. 45F-H)—   **2**

2   Antennal ratio 0·4-0·6.   Hypopygium as in fig. 134D—
                                   P. penerasus (Edwards)

—   Antennal ratio 0·7-1·1—   **3**

3   Anal point short, pubescent (fig. 45G).   Hypopygium fig. 135A—
                                   P. irritus (Walker)

—   Anal point longer, apical portion bare (fig. 45H).   Hypopygium fig.
    135B—   **P. impensus** (Walker)

One other British species, *Paraphaenocladius cuneatus* (Edwards) is known only from the
female.

Genus PARATRISSOCLADIUS Zavrel

Only one British species is referred here, the hypopygium of which is
distinctive (fig. 135C)—   **Paratrissocladius excerptus** (Walker)

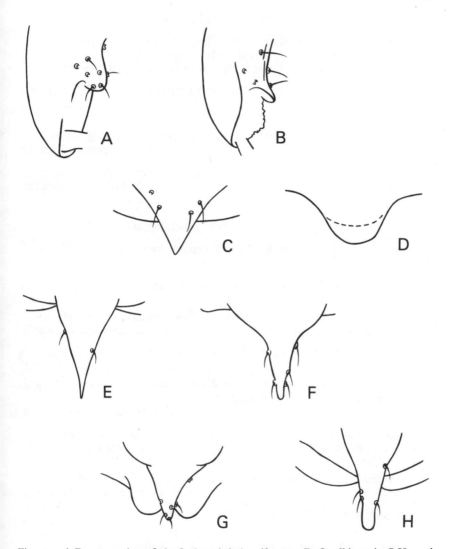

Fig. 45 A-B, gonocoxites of: A, *Orthosmittia brevifurcata*; B, *O. albipennis*; C-H, anal points of: C, *Parakiefferiella bathophila*; D, *P. coronata*; E, *Paraphaenocladius* sp.a; F, *Paraphaenocladius penerasus*; G, *P. irritus*; H, *P. impensus*.

Genus PSEUDORTHOCLADIUS Goetghebuer

1   Antennal ratio only about 0·7.   Ground colour of thorax yellowish.
    Wing length *c.* 1·4 mm.   Hypopygium fig. 135D—
                    Pseudorthocladius curtistylus (Goetghebuer)

—   Antennal ratio 1·0 or more.   Thorax entirely black.   Wing length *c.*
    2·0 mm—   **2**

2   Lobe of gonocoxite rounded (fig. 46A).   Hypopygium fig. 136A—
                                    P. pilosipennis Brundin

—   Lobe of gonocoxite somewhat angular (fig. 46B).   Hypopygium fig.
    136B—   **P. filiformis** (Kieffer)

Genus PSEUDOSMITTIA (Goetghebuer)

1   Gonocoxite with three lobes, two ventral and one dorsal (fig. 46C-
    E)—   **2**

—   Gonocoxite with one or two lobes only (fig. 46F-H)—   **4**

2   Dorsal lobe of gonocoxite slender, foot-shaped distally (fig. 46C).
    Hypopygium fig. 136C—   **Pseudosmittia trilobata** (Edwards)

—   Dorsal lobe broader (fig. 46D-E)—   **3**

3   The more anterior of the ventral lobes about six times as long as
    broad (fig. 46D).   Hypopygium fig. 136D—
                            P. forcipata (Goetghebuer)

—   Anterior ventral lobe about twice as long as broad (fig. 46E).
    Hypopygium fig. 137A—   **P. angusta** (Edwards)

4(1) Antennal ratio very low, about 0·3 or less.   Hypopygium fig.
    137B—   **P. gracilis** (Goetghebuer)

—   Antennal ratio at least 0·6—   **5**

5   Anal point very short (fig. 46I).   Antennal ratio *c.* 0·6.
    Hypopygium fig. 137C—   **P. recta** (Edwards)

—   Anal point well developed (fig. 46J).   Antennal ratio *c.* 1·0.
    Hypopygium fig. 137D—   **P. curticosta** (Edwards)

Two other species, *P. conjuncta* (Edwards) and *P. scotica* (Edwards) are known only from
the females.

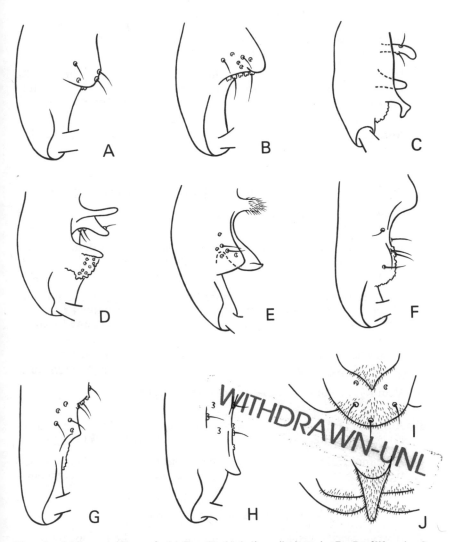

Fig. 46 A-H, gonocoxites of: A, *Pseudorthocladius pilosipennis*; B, *P. filiformis*; C, *Pseudosmittia trilobata*; D, *P. forcipata*; E, *P. angusta*; F, *P. gracilis*; G, *P. recta*; H, *P. curticosta*; I-J, anal points of: I, *P. recta*; J, *P. curticosta*.

Genus SMITTIA Holmgren

I Inner margin of gonostylus strongly expanded subapically (fig. 47 C-
   F).   Gonocoxite lobe not as in fig. 47B—   **2**

— Inner expansion of gonostylus less pronounced (fig. 47A).
   Gonocoxite lobe characteristically shaped (fig. 47B).   Hypopygium
   fig. 138A—   **Smittia contingens** (Walker)

2 Antennal ratio *c.* 2·5.   Hypopygium fig. 138B—**S. foliacea** (Kieffer)

— Antennal ratio <2·0—   **3**

3 Anal point short, microtrichia extending almost to apex (fig. 47G)—**4**

— Anal point longer, distal half bare (fig. 47H)—   **5**

4 Inner margin of gonostylus expanded distally, for less than a quarter
   of its total length (fig. 47D).   Antennal ratio 1·0-1·3.   Hypopygium
   fig. 138C—   **S. leucopogon** (Meigen)

— Inner expansion of gonostylus more extensive, occupying roughly half
   of the total length of the gonostylus (fig. 47E).   Antennal ratio 1·5-
   2·0.   Hypopygium fig. 138D—   **S. aterrima** (Meigen)

5(3) Vein R_{4+5} ending above, or just beyond, tip of vein Cu_1 (fig.
     47I).   Hypopygium fig. 139A—   **S. pratorum** (Goetghebuer)

—   Vein R_{4+5} ending proximal to tip of vein Cu_1 (fig. 47J-K)—   **6**

6 Antennal ratio 1·4-1·6.   Anal lobe of wing obtuse (fig. 47J).
   Hypopygium fig. 139B—   **S. edwardsi** Goetghebuer

— Antennal ratio 1·0-1·2.   Anal lobe absent (fig. 47K).   Hypopygium
   fig. 139C—   **S. nudipennis** (Goetghebuer)

Genus THALASSOSMITTIA Strenzke

A monospecific genus, easily recognizable from the hypopygium (fig.
139D).   A coastal species—
                          Thalassosmittia thalassophila (Goetghebuer)

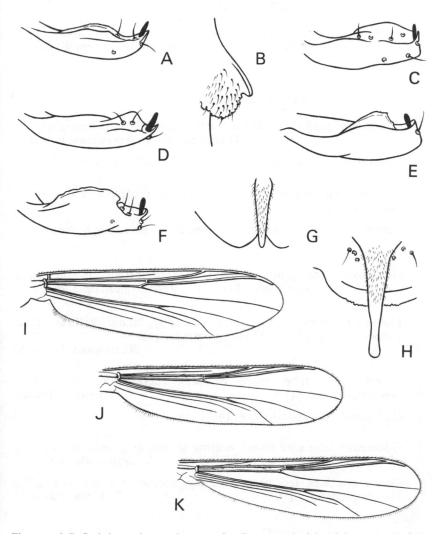

Fig. 47 A-B, *Smittia contingens*; A, gonostylus; B, gonocoxite lobe; C-F, gonostyli of: C, *S. foliacea*; D, *S. leucopogon*; E, *S. aterrima*, F, *S. pratorum*; G-H, anal points of: G, *S. leucopogon*; H, *S. pratorum*; I-K, wings of: I, *S. pratorum*; J, *S. edwardsi*; K, *S. nudipennis*.

Genus THIENEMANNIA Kieffer

A monospecific genus. Antennal ratio only about 0·3. Hypopygium as in fig. 140A—   **Thienemannia gracilis** Kieffer

Genus THIENEMANNIELLA Kieffer

1   Gonocoxite without a distinct lobe (fig. 48A). Hypopygium fig. 140B—   **Thienemanniella flavescens** (Edwards)

—   Gonocoxite with a well developed inner lobe (fig. 48B-F)—   **2**

2   Last antennal segment only as long as preceding 2-3 segments combined—   **3**

—   Last antennal segment at least as long as the preceding 6 combined—
                                                                       4

3   Gonocoxite lobe gently rounded, tapered distally and extending almost to end of gonocoxite (fig. 48B). Hypopygium fig. 140C—
                                              T. clavicornis (Kieffer)

—   Gonocoxite lobe ending rather abruptly, about halfway along gonocoxite (fig. 48C). Hypopygium fig. 140D—
                                                 T. morosa (Edwards)

4(2) Gonocoxite lobe more or less rectangular (fig. 48D). Hypopygium fig. 141A—   **T. vittata** (Edwards)

—   Gonocoxite lobe rounded (fig. 48E-F)—   **5**

5   Gonocoxite lobe very broad, bearing several long setae dorsally (fig. 48E). Hypopygium fig. 141B—   **T. majuscula** (Edwards)

—   Gonocoxite lobe less broad, bearing microtrichia only (fig. 48F). Hypopygium fig. 141C—   **T. lutea** (Edwards)

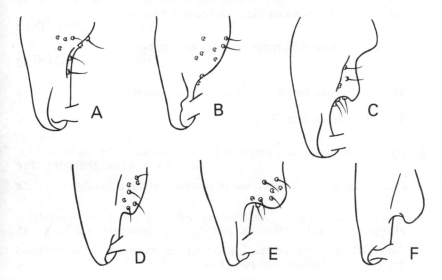

Fig. 48   Gonocoxites of: A, *Thienemanniella flavescens*; B, *T. clavicornis*; C, *T. morosa*;
D, *T. vittata*; E, *T. majuscula*; F, *T. lutea*.

CHIRONOMINAE

KEY TO GENERA

1 Wing membrane usually lacking macrotrichia.   If macrotrichia are present then the squama (fig. 5) is fringed with setae—
Tribe CHIRONOMINI **2**

— Wing membrane with macrotrichia, squama bare—
Tribe TANYTARSINI **33**

2 Wing membrane bearing macrotrichia towards the tip—   **3**

— Wing membrane bare—   **6**

3 Appendage 2 extremely broad and bulbous apically (fig. 49A)—
KIEFFERULUS Goetghebuer p. 126

— Appendage 2 more slender, not or scarcely enlarged distally—   **4**

4 Antennal ratio *c*. 3·0.   Anterior leg ratio only about 1·0. Gonostylus abruptly rounded distally (fig. 49B)—   SERGENTIA Kieffer p. 138

— Antennal ratio 2·0 or less.   Anterior leg ratio >1·2.   Gonostylus more tapered distally (fig. 49C-D)—   **5**

5 Antennal ratio *c*. 2·0.   Posterior tibia usually with 2 short apical spurs (fig. 49E) (occasionally only one is present).   Gonostylus without long setae on inner side except at tip (fig. 49C)—
PHAENOPSECTRA Kieffer p. 134

— Antennal ratio *c*. 1·0.   Posterior tibiae with a single, long, apical spur.   Gonostylus with several long inner setae (fig. 49D)—
PENTAPEDILUM Kieffer p. 134

6(2) All tibiae with long conspicuous spurs (fig. 49G-H).   Eyes kidney shaped, without long dorsal projections—
PSEUDOCHIRONOMUS Malloch p. 138

— Anterior tibiae with spurs very small or absent.   Eyes strongly produced dorsally (cf. fig. 3A)—   **7**

7 Combs of posterior tibiae composed of very short free spinules, without any indication of a spur (fig. 49F)—
GRACEUS Goetghebuer p. 124

— Combs of posterior tibiae composed of basally fused spinules, and with at least one distinct spur (e.g. fig. 49E)—   **8**

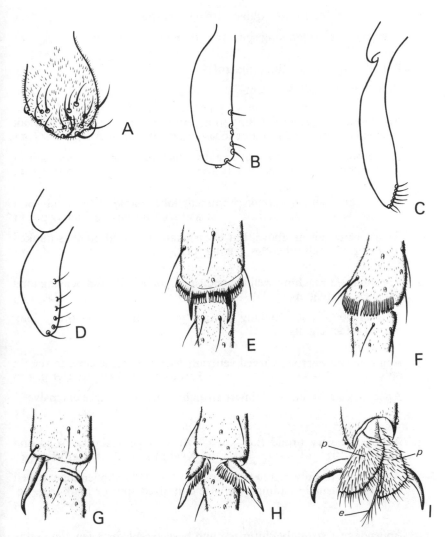

Fig. 49   A, appendage 2 of *Kiefferulus tendipediformis*; B-E, gonostyli of: B, *Sergentia coracina*; C, *Phaenopsectra flavipes*; D, *Pentapedilum sordens*; E-F, posterior tibial combs of: E, *Phaenopsectra flavipes*; F, *Graceus ambiguus*; G-H, *Pseudochironomus prasinatus*; G, anterior tibial spur; H, posterior tibial spurs; I, foot of *Chironomus salinarius*.
(*p* = pulvillus, *e* = empodium).

8   Both combs of posterior tibiae with a short spur—   **9**

—   One comb bearing a long spur, the other without a spur—   **27**

9   Pulvilli large and distinct (fig. 49I)—   **10**

—   Pulvilli very small or absent—   **26**

10   Antepronotum large, reaching to anterior margin of scutum, and not completely separated into two lobes anteriorly (fig. 50A-B)—   **11**

—   Antepronotum reduced, not usually reaching to anterior margin of scutum, but if so it is completely divided into two anterior lobes—   **23**

11   Anal tergite with a pair of prominent lobes flanking the anal point (fig. 50C)—   CAMPTOCHIRONOMUS Kieffer p. 111

—   Anal tergite not as above, but occasionally the anal point is flanked by a pair of small tubercles (e.g. fig. 51F)—   **12**

12   Appendage 2 reaching well beyond tip of gonocoxite and bearing long curved setae (e.g. fig. 50D)—   **13**

—   Appendage 2 not reaching beyond gonocoxite and without long curved setae (e.g. fig. 51C,E)—   **16**

13   Appendage 2 narrow, curved ventrally with long setae close to the tip only (fig. 50D)—   LIMNOCHIRONOMUS Kieffer p. 126

—   Appendage 2 broad and almost straight, long setae more extensive—   **14**

14   Anal point very broad (fig. 50E). Appendage 1 short, broad and pubescent (fig. 50F)—   XENOCHIRONOMUS Kieffer p. 140

—   Anal point usually narrower (e.g. fig. 50G-H). Appendage 1 well developed, usually ending in a bare chitinized spur or hook (e.g. fig. 50I-J)—   **15**

15   Appendage 1 strongly chitinized and bare except for a few long setae basally (e.g. fig. 50I)—   CHIRONOMUS Meigen p. 111

—   Basal half, at least, of appendage 1 pubescent (e.g. fig. 50J)—   EINFELDIA Kieffer p. 120

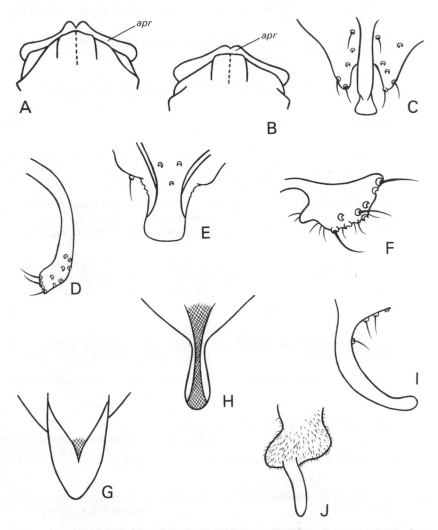

Fig. 50 A-B, dorsal views of anterior of thorax to show the antepronotum (*apr*) of: A, *Camptochironomus tentans*; B, *Chironomus salinarius*; C, anal tergite of *Camptochironomus pallidivittatus*; D, lateral view of appendage 2 of *Limnochironomus pulsus*; E-F, *Xenochironomus xenolabis*: E, anal point; F, appendage 1; G-H, anal points of: G, *Chironomus obtusidens*; H, *C. aprilinus*; I-J, appendage 1 of: I, *Chironomus anthracinus*; J, *Einfeldia pagana*.

16(12) Appendage 1 rod-like, of variable length and bearing a few apical setae (e.g. fig. 51A-B)—　　　　　　　　　　　　　　　　　**17**

—　Appendage 1 in the form of a short, broad pubescent pad (fig. 51C-D) or sometimes reduced or absent—　　　　　　　　　　　**19**

17　Appendage 2 in the form of a small pubescent pad (e.g. fig. 51E)—
　　　　　　　　　　　　　　　　PARACHIRONOMUS Lenz p. 130

—　Appendage 2 absent—　　　　　　　　　　　　　　　　　　**18**

18　Gonostylus long, strongly incurved and swollen basally with an apical tooth (fig. 51B). On each side of the anal point is a short tubercle bearing several setae (fig. 51F)— LEPTOCHIRONOMUS Pagast p. 126

—　Gonostylus long and incurved but not much swollen basally, without an apical tooth (fig. 51G). Anal tergite without processes next to the anal point—　　　　　　　　CRYPTOTENDIPES Lenz p. 120

19(16) Appendage 2 in the form of a small pubescent pad (fig. 51C). Appendage 1 short and broad, densely pubescent with a few long setae (fig. 51C)—　　　　PARACLADOPELMA Harnisch p. 132

—　Appendages not as above—　　　　　　　　　　　　　　　**20**

20　Gonostylus short and broad (fig. 51H). Appendage 1 short, broad and pubescent (fig. 51D)— CRYPTOCHIRONOMUS Kieffer p. 116

—　Gonostylus longer (e.g. fig. 51I-L). Appendage 1 strongly reduced or absent—　　　　　　　　　　　　　　　　　　　**21**

21　Gonostylus with a dorsal keel (fig. 51I)
　　　　　　　　　　　　DEMICRYPTOCHIRONOMUS Lenz p. 120

—　Gonostylus without a keel dorsally (e.g. fig. 51J-L)—　　　　**22**

22　Gonostylus of uniform thickness or gently tapered from base to tip (fig. 51J-K)—　　　　　　　HARNISCHIA Kieffer p. 124

—　Gonostylus of varying thickness and abruptly curved in distal half (fig. 51L)—　　　　　CRYPTOCLADOPELMA Lenz p. 118

23(10) Antepronotum extending to anterior edge of scutum but deeply divided into two anterior lobes—　　　　　　　　　　**24**

—　Antepronotum reduced, not reaching to front edge of scutum—　**25**

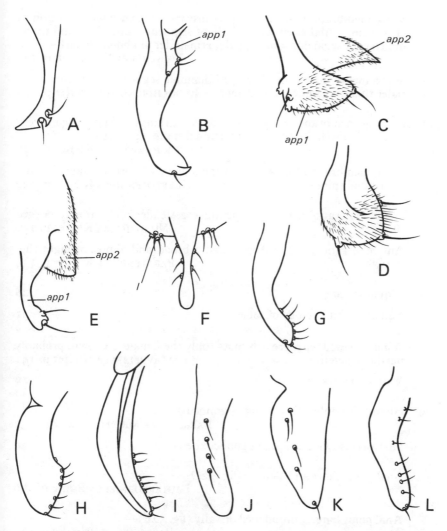

Fig. 51   A, appendage 1 of *Parachironomus monochromus*; B, gonostylus and appendage
1 of *Leptochironomus tener*; C, appendages 1 and 2 of *Paracladopelma
laminata*; D, appendage 1 of *Cryptochironomus rostratus*; E, appendages 1 and
2 of *Parachironomus frequens*; F, anal point and lateral lobes (*l*) of
Leptochironomus deribae; G-L, gonostyli of: G, *Cryptotendipes nigronitens*; H,
Cryptochironomus redekei; I, *Demicryptochironomus vulneratus*; J, *Harnischia
curtilamellata*, K, *H. fuscimana*; L, *Cryptocladopelma viridula*.

24 Wing membrane with a broad, transverse, brown band in region of cross-vein. Abdomen with whole of segment 1 and the distal three-quarters of segments 3 and 4 pale, remainder of abdomen dark— DEMEIJEREA Kruseman p. 120

— Wing membrane unmarked. Abdominal segments 1, 3 and 4 not paler than remainder of abdomen— ENDOCHIRONOMUS Kieffer p. 122

25(23) Wing membrane with distinct dark markings. Appendage 2 very long with a well differentiated terminal spine (fig. 52A)— STENOCHIRONOMUS Kieffer p. 140

— Wing membrane unmarked. Appendage 2 of normal shape, lacking a terminal spine— GLYPTOTENDIPES Kieffer p. 122

26(9) Antennal ratio c. 0·3. Appendage 2 slender and strongly curved (fig. 52B)— NILOTHAUMA Kieffer p. 130

— Antennal ratio >1·0. Appendage 2 broad and almost straight (fig. 52C)— PARATENDIPES Kieffer p. 134

27(8) Squama bare— 28

— Squama with a fringe of setae— 31

28 Wings covered with greyish spots (only the female is known, probably parthenogenetic)— ZAVRELIELLA Kieffer p. 141

— Wings unmarked— 29

29 Gonostylus only half as long as gonocoxite— PARALAUTERBORNIELLA Lenz p. 132

— Gonostylus twice as long as gonocoxite— 30

30 Anal point short and slender (fig. 52D)— LAUTERBORNIELLA Bause p. 126

— Anal point longer, broadened distally (fig. 52E)— PAGASTIELLA Brundin p. 130

31(27) Scutum with a small dorsal tubercle (fig. 52F). Wing membrane with distinct dark markings but sometimes only a single dark patch is present, in the region of r-m. Legs usually distinctly ringed— STICTOCHIRONOMUS Kieffer p. 140

— Scutum without a dorsal hump. Wing membrane marked or not. Legs not ringed— 32

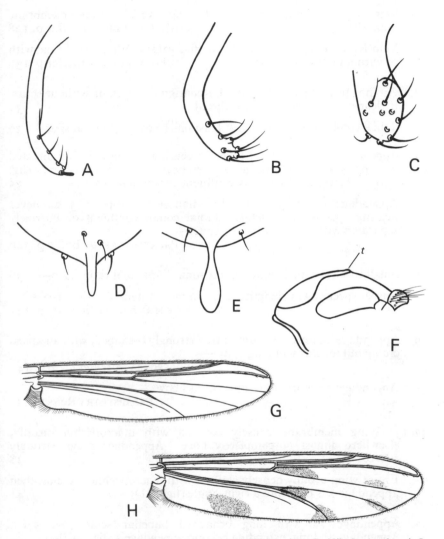

Fig. 52 A-C, appendage 2 of: A, *Stenochironomus hibernicus*; B, *Nilothauma brayi*; C, *Paratendipes albimanus*; D-E, anal points of: D, *Lauterborniella agrayloides*; E, *Pagastiella orophila*; F, lateral view of scutum of *Stictochironomus pictulus*, showing median 'tubercle' (*t*); G-H, wings of: G, *Microtendipes pedellus*; H, *Polypedilum laetum*.

32 Vein R_{2+3} ending close to R_1 (fig. 52G). Wing membrane unmarked— MICROTENDIPES Kieffer p. 128

— Vein R_{2+3} ending well distal to R_1 (fig. 52H). Wing membrane with or without dark markings— POLYPEDILUM Kieffer p. 136

33(1) Combs of posterior tibia usually contiguous, with or without spurs. If clearly separated, spurs are absent— **34**

— Tibial combs well separated, at least one bearing a longish spur— **37**

34 Appendage 1 with a basal tubercle bearing a long medially directed seta (fig. 53A). Appendage 2a often bearing spoon-shaped setae (fig. 53B). Tibial combs usually confluent and without spurs— **35**

— Appendage 1 without a basal-median seta. Appendage 2a never bearing spoon-shaped setae. Tibial combs confluent or narrowly separated with one or two short spurs— PARATANYTARSUS Bause p. 146

35 Small species, wing length 1·0-2·4 mm. Antennal ratio $<1·0$— **36**

— Larger species, wing length 2·0-4·0 mm. Antennal ratio $>1·0$— MICROPSECTRA Kieffer (in part) p. 142

36 Appendage 2a long (>45 μm), often strongly S-shaped, with an apical clump of lamellar setae (fig. 53C)— MICROPSECTRA (*attenuata* gp) p. 142

— Appendage 2a short (<40 μm), not as above— PARAPSECTRA Reiss p. 145

37(33) Wing membrane densely covered with macrotrichia distally, elsewhere almost or completely bare. Appendage 2 not strongly curved— **38**

— Entire wing usually densely clothed with macrotrichia. If not, then appendage 2 is bent into a right-angle (fig. 53D)— **41**

38 Appendage 2a with long branched lamellar setae (fig. 53E). Appendage 1a long, extending beyond appendage 1 (fig. 53F)— CLADOTANYTARSUS Kieffer p. 142

— Appendage 2a not as above, 1a absent— **39**

39 Eyes pubescent (cf. fig. 3B)— ZAVRELIA Kieffer p. 158

— Eyes bare— **40**

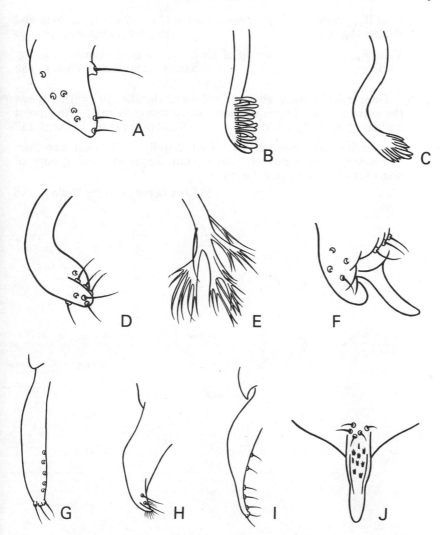

Fig. 53   A, appendage 1 of *Micropsectra junci*; B-C, appendage 2a of: B, *M. bidentata*;
C, *M. attenuata*; D, appendage 2 of *Tanytarsus sylvaticus*; E, appendage 2a of
Cladotanytarsus mancus; F, appendages 1 and 1a of *C. vanderwulpi*; G-I,
gonostyli of: G, *Stempellina bausei*; H, *Stempellinella brevis*; I, *Rheotanytarsus
pentapoda*; J, anal point of *Tanytarsus pallidicornis*.

40   Vein R_{4+5} ending well proximal to tip of Cu_1.   Gonostylus long and
      slender (fig. 53G)—   STEMPELLINA Bause p. 150

—   Vein R_{4+5} ending above tip of Cu_1.   Gonostylus shorter (e.g. fig.
      53H)—   STEMPELLINELLA Brundin p. 150

41(37) Gonostylus usually abruptly narrowed distally (fig. 53I).   If not
      the antennal flagellum is composed of 12 segments only.   Anal point
      without groups of dark spines—   RHEOTANYTARSUS Bause p. 148

—   Gonostylus not abruptly narrowed distally.   Antennal flagellum
      composed of 13 segments.   Anal point frequently with groups of
      short spines dorsally (e.g. fig. 53J)—

                                        TANYTARSUS van der Wulp p. 150

KEYS TO SPECIES

Tribe CHIRONOMINI
Genus Camptochironomus Kieffer

1 The lobes flanking the anal point relatively short (fig. 54A). Gonostylus relatively slender (fig. 54C). Hypopygium fig. 142A— **Camptochironomus tentans** (Fabricius)

— Lobes longer (fig. 54B). Gonostylus more robust (fig. 54D). Hypopygium fig. 142B— **C. pallidivittatus** (Malloch)

Genus Chironomus Meigen
(Strenzke 1959)

In section, the anal point of *Chironomus* is roughly T-shaped, since the dorsal keels are expanded into broad lamellae. In the figures of *Chironomus* hypopygia the ventral contours are cross-hatched in order to distinguish the dorsal lamellae from the more ventral parts.

1 Anal point parallel-sided or tapered from base to tip (e.g. fig. 54E-G)—   **2**

— Anal point constricted basally and expanded in distal half (fig. 54H)—   **10**

2 Anal point very broad (fig. 54E-F)—   **3**

— Anal point more slender (e.g. fig. 54G)—   **4**

3 Anal point tapered to a point distally (fig. 54E). Hypopygium fig. 142C— **Chironomus obtusidens** Goetghebuer

— Anal point broadly rounded distally (fig. 54F). Hypopygium fig. 142D— **Chironomus sp. a**

The two specimens referred here from the British Museum (Natural History) collection were previously identified as **C. striatus** Strenzke (Kloet & Hincks 1975). However, the hypopygium differs from that figured by Strenzke (1959) in having a very broad appendage 2.

4(2) Frontal tubercles (cf. fig. 3A) minute (<10 μm long) or absent. Hypopygium fig. 143A— **Chironomus inermifrons** Goetghebuer

— Frontal tubercles well developed (> 30 μm long)— **5**

5 Anterior tarsus with a long beard. Beard ratio (see p. 11) >4·5 (fig. 54I)— **6**

— Anterior tarsus with beard short (Beard ratio <4·0) or absent (fig. 54J)— **8**

6 Entirely black. Beard ratio 4·5-5·7. Hypopygium fig. 143B— **C. anthracinus** Zetterstedt

— Not entirely black, abdominal tergites with pale posterior borders, or more extensively pale. Beard ratio >6·0— **7**

7 Abdomen greenish, tergites 2-4 sometimes with a small dark median spot. Hypopygium fig. 143C— **C. prasinus** Meigen su. Edwards (*C. plumosus* var. *prasinus* Mg., Edwards 1929)

Although Edwards regarded *prasinus* as a variety of *C. plumosus* the hypopygia of the two species are distinct (cf. fig. 145C).

— Abdomen mainly dark brown but tergites with narrowly pale posterior borders. Wing length 6·0-6·3 mm. Antennal ratio 4·6-5·2. Hypopygium fig. 143D—**C. annularius** (Degeer) su. Edwards

C. annularius Meigen, sensu Strenzke 1959 is a much smaller species (wing length *c.* 4·0 mm) with a lower antennal ratio (*c.* 4·0).

8(5) Appendage 1 tapered to a point distally (fig. 55A). Hypopygium fig. 144A— **C. cingulatus** Meigen

— Appendage 1 roughly parallel-sided and broadly rounded distally (fig. 55B-C)— **9**

9 Appendage 1 slightly curved, not darker than the rest of the hypopygium (fig. 55B). Hypopygium fig. 144B— **C. venustus** Staeger (*C. dorsalis* var. *venustus* Staeg., Edwards 1929)

Although *C. venustus* was regarded as a variety of *C. dorsalis* by Edwards 1929, the hypopygia of the two species are quite distinct (cf. fig. 145A).

— Appendage 1 strongly curved and distinctly darker than the remainder of the hypopygium (fig. 55C). Hypopygium fig. 144C— **C. longistylus** Goetghebuer

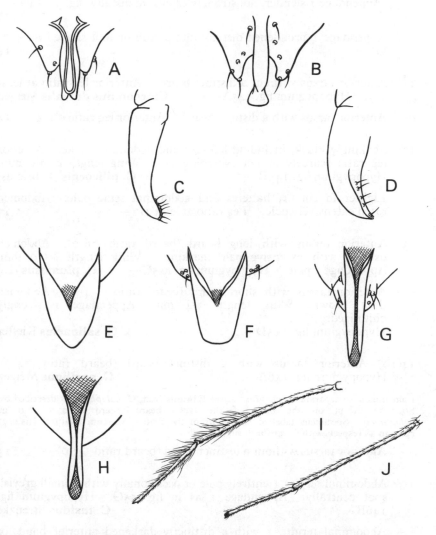

Fig. 54   A-B, anal tergites of: A, *Camptochironomus tentans*; B, *C. pallidivittatus*; C-D, gonostyli of: C, *C. tentans*; D, *C. pallidivittatus*; E-H, anal points of: E, *Chironomus obtusidens*; F, *Chironomus* sp.a; G, *C. prasinus*; H, *C. plumosus*; I-J, anterior tarsal beards of: I, *C. anthracinus*; J, *C. venustus*.

10(1) Appendage 1 slender, not strongly expanded distally (fig. 55D-E)—
                                                                    11

— Appendage 1 broadened distally into a club or foot shape (fig. 55F-G)—
                                                                    14

11 Anterior tarsus without a distinct beard.   Anterior leg ratio at least
   1·5. Hypopygium fig. 145A—   **Chironomus dorsalis** Meigen

— Anterior tarsus with a distinct beard.   Anterior leg ratio <1·4— 12

12 Strikingly black, including halteres and abdominal setae.   Anterior
   leg ratio scarcely or not exceeding 1·0.   Wing length c. 6·0 mm.
   Hypopygium fig. 145B—   **C. pilicornis** (Fabricius)

— Lighter in colour, halteres and abdominal setae pale.   Abdomen
   often extensively pale.   Leg ratio at least 1·2—   13

13 Anterior tarsus with long beard (beard ratio >6·0).   Abdomen
   usually with extensive pale markings.   Wing length >5·0 mm.
   Appendage 1 pale.   Hypopygium fig. 145C—   **C. plumosus** (L.)

— Anterior tarsus with short beard (beard ratio c. 4·5).   Abdomen
   dark brown.   Wing length 3-4 mm.   Appendage 1 strongly
   chitinized.
   Hypopygium fig. 145D—   **C. salinarius** Kieffer

14(10) Anterior tarsus with a distinct beard (beard ratio >4·5).
   Hypopygium fig. 146A—   **C. aprilinus** Meigen

I am unable to separate C. aprilinus sensu Edwards from C. halophilus as described by
Strenzke except on the basis of the tarsal beard (beard ratio c. 7·0 in
halophilus). Specimens labelled halophilus in the British Museum (Natural History)
agree in all respects with C. aprilinus su. Edwards.

— Anterior tarsus without a distinct beard (beard ratio <3·0)—   15

15 Abdominal tergite 1 entirely pale or occasionally with a small greyish
   spot centrally.   Appendage 1 as in fig. 55G.   Hypopygium fig.
   146B—   **C. luridus** Strenzke

— Abdominal tergite 1 with a distinctly darkened anterior band, or
   entirely dark brown.   Appendage 1 strongly expanded distally (fig.
   55F)—   16

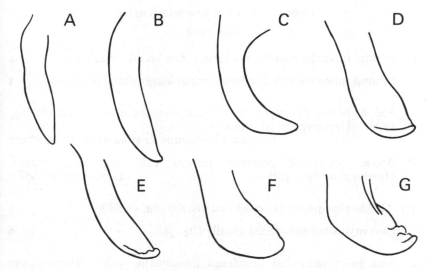

Fig. 55 A–G, appendage 1 of: A, *Chironomus cingulatus*; B, *C. venustus*; C, *C. longistylus*; D, *C. dorsalis*; E, *C. plumosus*; F, *C. riparius*; G, *C. luridus*.

16   Entirely blackish brown.   Hypopygium fig. 146C—
                                                          C. lugubris Zetterstedt
This may be no more than a dark form of *C. riparius*.

—   Abdomen with pale bands—   **17**

17   Anterior leg ratio 1·3–1·5.   Hypopygium fig. 146D—
                                                          C. riparius Meigen

—   Anterior leg ratio >1·55.   Hypopygium as in *C. riparius*—
                                                          C. pseudothummi Strenzke

Genus Cryptochironomus Kieffer
(Reiss 1968)

1 Frontal tubercles minute, not longer than broad, or absent—   **2**

— Frontal tubercles well developed, much longer than broad—   **3**

2 Apical hooks of posterior femora conspicuously darkened (fig. 56A). Hypopygium fig. 147A—
    Cryptochironomus denticulatus Goetghebuer

— Apical hooks of posterior femora pale and inconspicuous. Hypopygium fig. 147B—   **C. rostratus** Kieffer

3(1) Gonostylus distinctly broadened distally (fig. 56B-D)—   **4**

— Gonostylus not broadened distally (fig. 56E)—   **6**

4 Anal point somewhat broadened distally (fig. 56F). Hypopygium fig. 147C—   **C. supplicans** (Meigen)

— Anal point tapered (fig. 56G)—   **5**

5 Outer margin of appendage 1 distinctly notched (fig. 56K). Entirely dark brown in colour. Hypopygium fig. 147D—
    C. redekei (Kruseman)

— Outer margin of appendage 1 smoothly rounded (fig. 56J). Abdomen green, ground colour of thorax pale with dark brown scutal stripes. Hypopygium fig. 148A—   **C. psittacinus** (Meigen)

6(3) Anal point parallel-sided or slightly expanded distally (fig. 56H). Anterior tarsus with a distinct beard. Hypopygium fig. 148B—
    C. albofasciatus (Staeger)

— Anal point tapered (fig. 56I). Anterior tarsus without a beard. Hypopygium fig. 148C—   **C. obreptans** (Walker)

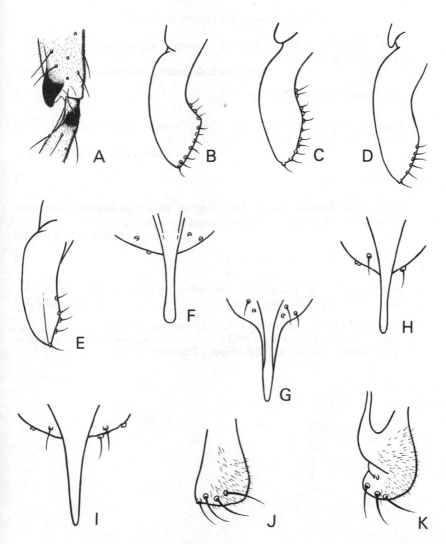

Fig. 56 A, tip of posterior femur of *Cryptochironomus denticulatus*; B-E, gonostyli of: B, *C. redekei*; C, *C. psittacinus*; D, *C. supplicans*; E, *C. albofasciatus*; F-I, anal points of: F, *C. supplicans*; G, *C. redekei*; H, *C. albofasciatus*; I, *C. obreptans*; J-K, appendages 1 of: J, *C. psittacinus*; K. *C. redekei*.

Genus CRYPTOCLADOPELMA Lenz

1 Anal tergite with wing-like lateral expansions (fig. 57A). Hypopygium fig. 148D—

Cryptocladopelma lateralis (Goetghebuer)

— Anal tergite not as above—   2

2 Base of anal point covered by a large median expansion of the anal tergite (fig. 57B). Hypopygium fig. 149A—

C. krusemani (Goetghebuer)

— Not as above—   3

3 Anal point flanked basally by a pair of swellings bearing numerous strong setae (fig. 57C). Hypopygium fig. 149B—

C. virescens (Meigen)

— Not as above—   4

4 Inner margin of gonostylus somewhat swollen in basal half (fig. 57D). Hypopygium fig. 149C—   **C. viridula** (L.)

— Inner margin of gonostylus smoothly curved, not swollen basally (fig. 57E). Hypopygium fig. 149D—   **C. edwardsi** Kruseman (*Chironomus virescens* (Mg.) Goet., Edwards 1929)

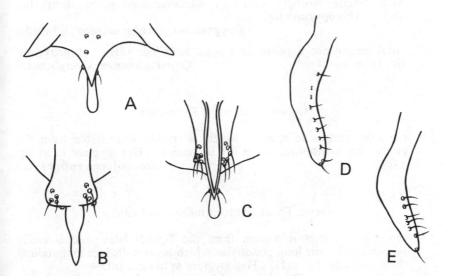

Fig. 57   A-C, anal tergites of: A, *Cryptocladopelma lateralis*; B, *C. krusemani*; C, *C. virescens*; D-E, gonostyli of: D, *C. viridula*; E, *C. edwardsi*.

Genus CRYPTOTENDIPES Lenz

1   Anal tergite strongly expanded dorsally, anal point short (fig.
     58A). Hypopygium fig. 150A—
                                    Cryptotendipes nigronitens (Edwards)

—   Anal tergite not swollen, anal point long (fig. 58B). Hypopygium
     fig. 150B—   **C. pseudotener** (Goetghebuer)

Genus DEMEIJEREA Kruseman

Contains only one species, which is readily identifiable from the
characters mentioned in the key to genera. Hypopygium as in fig.
150C—   **Demeijerea rufipes** (L.)

Genus DEMICRYPTOCHIRONOMUS Lenz

Only one species is known from the British Isles, and is easily
recognized by the long gonostylus which bears a distinct longitudinal
'keel' dorsally (fig. 51I). Hypopygium as in fig. 150D—
               Demicryptochironomus vulneratus (Zetterstedt)
(*Chironomus vulneratus* Zett., Edwards 1929)
(*Chironomus atriforceps* Goet., Edwards 1929)

Genus EINFELDIA Kieffer

1   Appendage 1 broad and pubescent basally, terminating in a bare rod-
     like process or 'hook' (e.g. fig. 58D)—   2

—   Appendage 1 broad and pubescent throughout (fig. 58C).
     Hypopygium fig. 151A—   **Einfeldia macani** (Freeman)

2   Anal point very broad (fig. 58E). Hypopygium fig. 151B—
                                             E. pagana (Meigen)

—   Anal point more slender, somewhat bulbous (fig. 58F)—   3

3   Outer margin of gonostylus swollen in basal half (fig. 58G).
     Hypopygium fig. 151C—   **E. longipes** (Staeger)

—   Gonostylus longer, not swollen basally (fig. 58H). Hypopygium fig.
     151D—   **E. dissidens** (Walker)

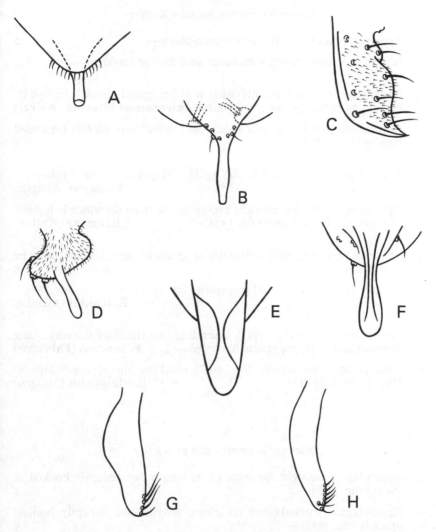

Fig. 58 A-B, anal points of: A, *Cryptotendipes nigronitens*; B, *C. pseudotener*; C-D, appendage 1 of: C, *Einfeldia macani*; D, *E. pagana*; E-F, anal points of: E, *E. pagana*; F, *E. longipes*; G-H, gonostyli of: G, *E. longipes*, H, *E. dissidens*.

Genus ENDOCHIRONOMUS Kieffer

1   Abdomen predominantly dark brown-black—   **2**

—   Abdomen mainly green, sometimes with darker markings—   **4**

2   Appendage 1 broad basally with a short apical 'hook' (fig. 59A).
     Hypopygium fig. 152A—   **Endochironomus intextus** (Walker)

—   Appendage 1 in the form of a long bare 'hook' only slightly expanded
     basally (fig. 59B-C)—   **3**

3   Appendage 1 robust, curved (fig. 59B).   Hypopygium fig. 152B—
                                                        E. dispar (Meigen)

—   Appendage 1 slender, straight except for extreme tip which is hooked
     (fig. 59C).   Hypopygium fig. 152C—   **E. impar** (Walker)

4(1) Thorax predominantly yellowish or greenish, scutal stripes may be
     darkened—   **5**

—   Thorax entirely black.   Hypopygium fig. 152D—
                                                       E. lepidus (Meigen)

5   Anal point slender (fig. 59D), extending two thirds of the way along
     appendage 2.   Hypopygium fig. 153A—   **E. tendens** (Fabricius)

—   Anal point more robust (fig. 59E) reaching tip of appendage 2.
     Hypopygium fig. 153B—   **E. albipennis** (Meigen)

Genus GLYPTOTENDIPES Kieffer

1   Appendage 1 straight for most of its length but abruptly hooked at
     the tip (fig. 59F)—   **2**

—   Appendage 1 curved over its entire length, not abruptly hooked
     apically (fig. 59G)—   **5**

2   Second segment of anterior tarsus distinctly shorter than third
     segment (fig. 59H).   Hypopygium fig. 153C—
                                        Glyptotendipes barbipes (Staeger)

—   Second segment of anterior tarsus equal to, or longer than, the
     third—   **3**

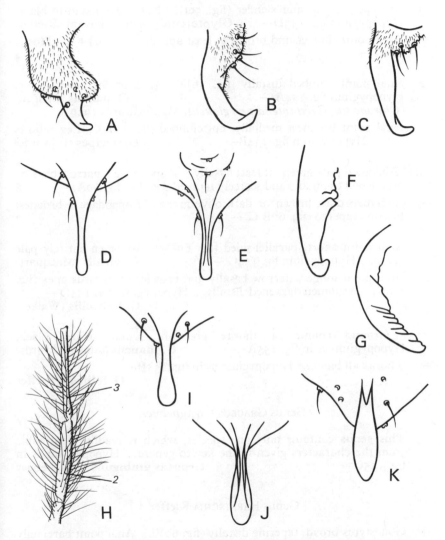

Fig. 59 A-C, appendages 1 of: A, *Endochironomus intextus*; B, *E. dispar*; C, *E. impar*,
D-E, anal points of: D, *E. tendens*; E, *E. albipennis*; F-G, appendages 1 of: F,
Glyptotendipes barbipes; G, *G. viridis*; H, second and third segments of anterior
tarsus of *G. barbipes;* I-K, anal points of: I, *G. gripekoveni*; J, *G. pallens*; K, *G.
paripes.*

3   Anal point long and slender (fig. 59I). Not predominantly black. Hypopygium fig. 153D—   **Glyptotendipes gripekoveni** (Kieffer)
—   Anal point shorter and broad, at least apically (fig. 59J-K). Mostly black—
                                           4

4   Anal point clubbed distally (fig. 59J). Anterior leg ratio $c.$ 1·5. Hypopygium fig. 154A—   **G. pallens** (Meigen) (*Chironomus (Glyptotendipes) glaucus*, Mg., Edwards 1929)
—   Anal point broadest medially, not clubbed (fig. 59K). Leg ratio $c.$ 1·2. Hypopygium fig. 154B—   **G. paripes** (Edwards)

5(1) Abdomen pale green, at least basally. Appendage 1 narrow basally, broadened to middle and scarcely tapered distally (fig. 60A)—   **6**
—   Abdomen dark brown or dark olive green. Appendage 1 broadest basally, tapered (fig. 60B-C)—   **7**

6   Anal point short, parallel-sided (fig. 60D). Abdomen entirely pale green. Hypopygium fig. 154C—   **G. viridis** (Macquart)
—   Anal point longer, narrow basally and broadened towards apex (fig. 60E). Abdomen darkened distally. Hypopygium fig. 154D—
                                    G. imbecilis (Walker)

7(5) Ground colour of thorax greenish, scutal stripes black. Hypopygium as in fig. 155A—   **G. mancunianus** (Edwards)
—   Thorax all black. Hypopygium as in fig. 155B—
                                    G. foliicola Kieffer

Genus GRACEUS Goetghebuer

This genus contains only one species, which is readily identifiable from the characters given in the key to genera. Hypopygium as in fig. 155C—   **Graceus ambiguus** Goetghebuer

Genus HARNISCHIA Kieffer

1   Gonostylus broad, tapering distally (fig. 60F). Anal point bare, only slightly broadened in distal half (fig. 60G). Hypopygium fig. 156A—   **Harnischia fuscimana** Kieffer
—   Gonostylus relatively slender, parallel-sided (fig. 60H). Anal point with several lateral setae and with a broad expansion distally (fig. 60I). Hypopygium fig. 156B—   **H. curtilamellata** (Malloch) (*Chironomus pseudosimplex* Goet., Edwards 1929)

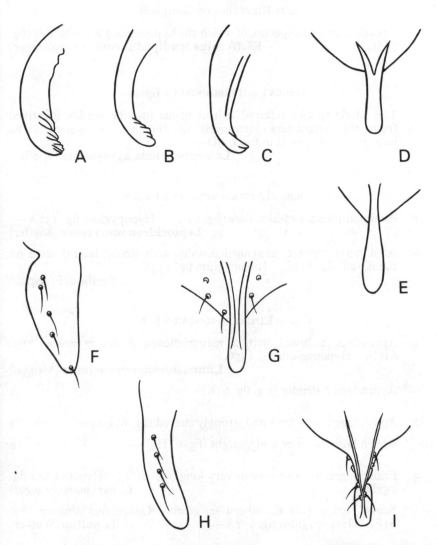

Fig. 60   A-C, appendages 1 of: A, *Glyptotendipes imbecilis*; B, *G. mancunianus*; C, *G. foliicola*; D-E, anal points of: D, *G. viridis*; E, *G. imbecilis*; F-G, *Harnischia fuscimana*: F, gonostylus; G, anal point; H-I, *H. curtilamellata*: H, gonostylus; I, anal point.

Genus KIEFFERULUS Goetghebuer

Contains only one species, of which the hypopygium is distinctive (fig. 156C)— **Kiefferulus tendipediformis** (Goetghebuer)

Genus LAUTERBORNIELLA Bause

The single species referred to this genus may be readily identified from the characters mentioned in the key to genera. The hypopygium is shown in fig. 156D—
Lauterborniella agrayloides (Kieffer)

Genus LEPTOCHIRONOMUS Pagast

1   Anal point long, rod-like, bare (fig. 61A). Hypopygium fig. 157A—
Leptochironomus tener (Kieffer)

—   Anal point shorter, expanded distally with strong lateral setae on basal half (fig. 61B). Hypopygium fig. 157B—
L. deribae (Freeman)

Genus LIMNOCHIRONOMUS Kieffer

1   Appendage 2 broad with a membraneous dorsal expansion (fig. 61C). Hypopygium fig. 157C—
Limnochironomus notatus (Meigen)

—   Appendage 2 slender (e.g. fig. 61E)—   **2**

2   Appendage 2 very long and strongly curved (fig. 61E,G)—   **3**

—   Appendage 2 shorter and straight (fig. 61H-J)—   **4**

3   Entirely green. Gonostylus very long (fig. 61D). Hypopygium fig. 157D—
L. nervosus (Staeger)

—   Scutal stripes black, otherwise green. Gonostylus shorter (fig. 61F). Hypopygium fig. 158A—
L. pulsus (Walker)

4(2) Appendage 2 bilobed apically (fig. 61H). Appendage 1 clubbed at tip (fig. 61I). Hypopygium fig. 158B—
L. tritomus (Kieffer)

—   Appendage 2 not bilobed (fig. 61J). Appendage 1 short, not clubbed but with a short, beak-like process (fig. 61K). Hypopygium fig. 158C—
L. lobiger (Kieffer)

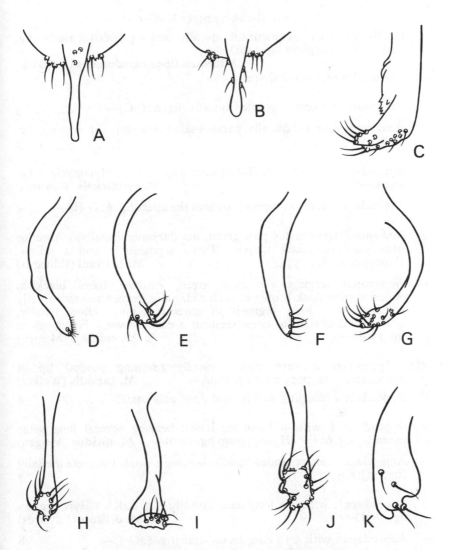

Fig. 61   A-B, anal points of: A, *Leptochironomus tener*; B, *L. deribae*; C, appendage 2 of
Limnochironomus notatus; D-E, *L. nervosus*; D, gonostylus: E, appendage 2; F-
G, *L. pulsus*; F, gonostylus; G, appendage 2; H-I, *L. tritomus*: H, appendage 2;
I, appendage 1; J-K, *L. lobiger*: J, appendage 2; K, appendage 1.

Genus MICROTENDIPES Kieffer

1   Gonostylus strongly incurved apically and expanded basally (fig. 62A). Hypopygium fig. 158D—
                          Microtendipes caledonicus (Edwards)
—   Gonostylus of normal shape   **2**

2   Anal point triangular, pointed apically (fig. 62B-C)—   **3**
—   Anal point rounded distally, parallel-sided or weakly tapered (e.g. fig. 62D-E)—   **5**

3   Appendage 1 broad, rounded apically (fig. 62F). Hypopygium fig. 159A—   **M. rydalensis** (Edwards)
—   Appendage 1 narrow, tapered towards the apex (fig. 62G-H)—   **4**

4   Abdominal tergites 1-5 pale green, not darkened basally. Anterior tibia uniformly dark brown. Tarsal segments 1 and 2 yellow. Hypopygium fig. 159C—   **M. britteni** (Edwards)
—   Abdominal tergites 1-5 olive green, extreme bases blackish. Anterior tibia dark brown at each end, paler (sometimes indistinctly so) medially. First segment of anterior tarsus yellow basally, gradually darkened to apex, segment 2 dark brown. Hypopygium fig. 159D—   **M. confinis** (Meigen)

5(2) Appendage 2 very short, scarcely reaching beyond tip of gonocoxite. Hypopygium fig. 160A—   **M. tarsalis** (Walker)
—   Appendage 2 reaching well beyond tip of gonocoxite—   **6**

6   Appendage 1 with a basal expansion bearing several long setae mesially (fig. 62I). Hypopygium fig. 160B—   **M. nitidus** (Meigen)
—   Appendage 1 not expanded basally, bearing a single long seta mesially (fig. 62J-K)—   **7**

7   Appendage 1 with 3-4 long setae dorsally (fig. 62K). Hypopygium fig. 160D—   **M. diffinis** (Edwards)
—   Appendage 1 with 5-10 long dorsal setae (fig. 62G-J)—   **8**

8   Abdominal segments 1-5 pale green, remainder black. Fore-tibiae pale medially, darkened at base and tip. Hypopygium fig. 159B—
                                                M. pedellus (Degeer)
—   Abdominal segments 1-5 dark green or blackish. Fore-tibiae blackish. Hypopygium fig. 160C—   **M. chloris** (Meigen)

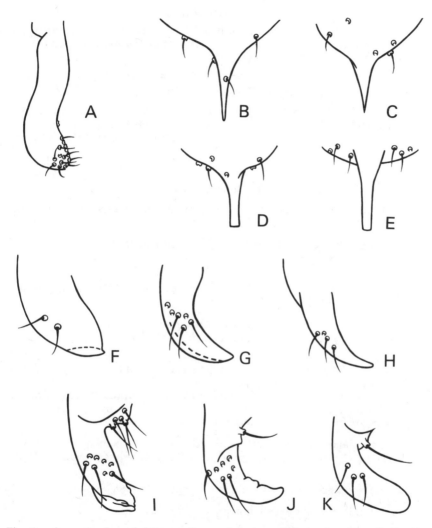

Fig. 62   A, gonostylus of *Microtendipes caledonicus*; B-E, anal points of: B, *M. rydalensis*; C, *M. confinis*; D, *M. tarsalis*; E, *M. chloris*; F-K, appendages 1 of: F, *M. rydalensis*; G, *M. pedellus*; H, *M. confinis*; I, *M. nitidus*; J, *M. chloris*; K, *M. diffinis*.

Genus NILOTHAUMA Kieffer

Contains a single species with a highly characteristic hypopygium (fig. 161A)— **Nilothauma brayi** (Goetghebuer) *(Kribioxenus brayi* G., Illies 1967)

Genus PAGASTIELLA Brundin

The single species belonging to this genus should be readily identified from the characters given in the key to genera. Hypopygium fig. 161B— **Pagastiella orophila** (Edwards)

Genus PARACHIRONOMUS Lenz
(Lehmann 1970)

1 At least one of the distal setae of appendage 1 arising from a large distinct pit (fig. 63A-B)— **2**

— Neither of the distal setae of appendage 1 arising from a distinct pit (fig. 63C-D)— **7**

2 Inner margin of gonostylus swollen in distal half before tapering to apex (fig. 63E-F)— **3**

— Gonostylus not as above, roughly parallel-sided or with outer margin somewhat expanded (fig. 63G-I)— **4**

3 Appendage 1 very long, distally produced into a beak-like process (fig. 63A). Hypopygium fig. 161C— **Parachironomus tenuicaudatus** (Malloch) *(Chironomus monochromus* (v.d.W.), Goet., Edwards 1929) *(Chironomus baciliger* Kieffer, Coe 1950)

— Appendage 1 shorter and differently shaped (fig. 63B). Hypopygium fig. 161D— **P. monochromus** (van der Wulp)

4(2) Appendage 1 with a distal-lateral process (fig. 63J-K)— **5**

— Appendage 1 lacking such a process (fig. 63L-M)— **6**

5 Gonostylus broadest about the middle of its length (fig. 63G). Hypopygium fig. 162A— **P. varus** Goetghebuer

In those British specimens which were examined the inner margin of appendage 1 is indented, whereas in Lehmann's (1970) figure this is shown as smoothly convex.

— Gonostylus broadest basally, uniformly tapering to tip (fig. 63H). Hypopygium fig. 162B— **P. parilis** (Walker)

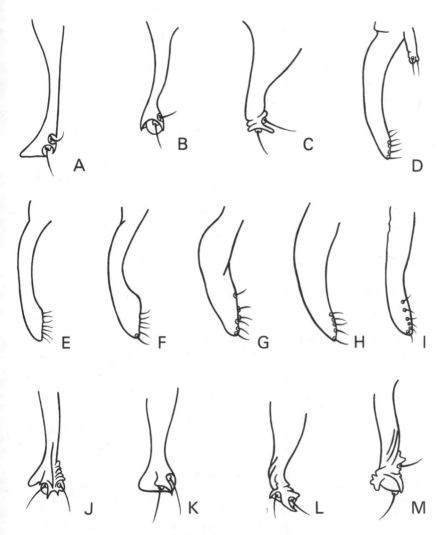

Fig. 63 A–C, appendages 1 of: A, *Parachironomus tenuicaudatus*; B, *P. monochromus*; C, *P. vitiosus*; D, gonostylus and appendage 1 of *P. arcuatus*; E–I, gonostyli of: E, *P. tenuicaudatus*; F, *P. monochromus*; G, *P. varus*; H, *P. parilis*; I, *P. digitalis*; J–M, appendages 1 of: J, *P. varus*; K, *P. parilis*; L, *P. biannulatus*; M, *P. digitalis*.

6(4) The distal seta of appendage 1 arises from a large pit, whereas the more proximal seta arises from a smaller pit (fig. 63M). Hypopygium fig. 162C—   **Parachironomus digitalis** (Edwards)

— The setae of appendage 1 arise from pits of similar size (fig. 63L). Hypopygium fig. 162D—   **P. biannulatus** (Staeger)

7(1) Gonostylus short and plump (fig. 64A). Hypopygium fig. 163A—
                                             P. vitiosus Goetghebuer

— Gonostylus long and slender (fig. 64B)—   **8**

8 Anal point broad, expanded distally (fig. 64C). Hypopygium fig. 163B—   **P. frequens** Malloch
   (*Chironomus longiforceps* Kieff., Edwards 1929)

— Anal point slender, not expanded distally (fig. 64D). Hypopygium fig. 163C—   **P. arcuatus** Goetghebuer

Genus PARACLADOPELMA Harnisch

1 Appendage 1 not expanded distally (fig. 64E). Gonostylus slightly constricted subapically (fig. 64F). Hypopygium fig. 163D—
                        Paracladopelma obscura Brundin

— Appendage 1 strongly expanded distally (fig. 64G-H). Gonostylus not constricted subapically (fig. 64I-J)—   **2**

2 Posterior median corner of appendage 2 produced into a fine point (fig. 64G). Hypopygium fig. 164A—   **P. laminata** Kieffer

— Appendage 2 broadly rounded posteriorly (fig. 64H). Hypopygium fig. 164B—   **P. camptolabis** Kieffer

Genus PARALAUTERBORNIELLA Lenz

Only one species is known which is easily identified from its distinctive hypopygium (fig. 164C)—
                        Paralauterborniella nigrohalteralis (Malloch)
(*Chironomus (Lauterborniella) brachylabis* Edwards 1929)

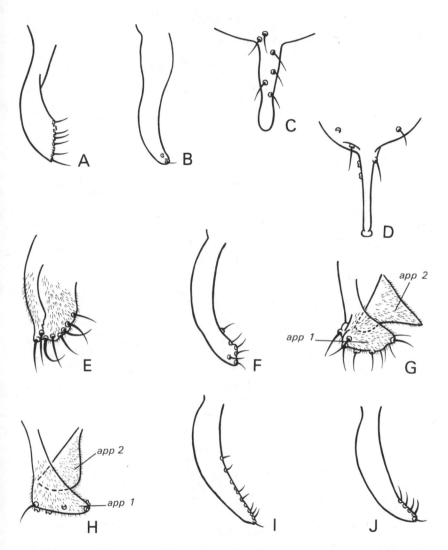

Fig. 64   A-B, gonostyli of: A, *Parachironomus vitiosus*; B, *P. frequens*; C-D, anal points of: C, *P. frequens*; D, *P. arcuatus*; E-F, *Paracladopelma obscura*: E, appendage 1; F, gonostylus; G-H, appendages 1 and 2 of: G, *P. laminata*; H, *P. camptolabis*; I-J, gonostyli of: I, *P. camptolabis*; J, *P. laminata*.

Genus PARATENDIPES Kieffer

1   Gonostylus broadened medially (fig. 65A). Anal point somewhat
expanded distally (fig. 65C). Hypopygium fig. 165A—
Paratendipes albimanus (Meigen)

—   Gonostylus slender, not broadened medially (fig. 65B). Anal point
parallel-sided or tapered towards apex (fig. 65D). Hypopygium fig.
165B— **P. nudisquama** (Edwards)

Genus PENTAPEDILUM Kieffer

1   Appendage 1 sickle-shaped without a long lateral seta (fig. 65E).
Hypopygium fig. 165C— **Pentapedilum nubens** (Edwards)

—   Appendage 1 not as above, bearing a long lateral seta (fig. 65F-H)—**2**

2   Gonostylus short and broad (fig. 65I). Lateral seta inserted about
one third of the way along appendage 1 (fig. 65F). Hypopygium fig.
165D— **P. sordens** (van der Wulp)

—   Gonostylus longer (fig. 65J-K). Lateral seta inserted at least
halfway along appendage 1 (fig. 65G-H)— **3**

3   Lateral seta inserted halfway along appendage 1 (fig. 65G). Anal
point slightly expanded distally and broadly rounded at apex (fig.
65L). Hypopygium fig. 166A— **P. tritum** (Walker)

—   Lateral seta inserted about two-thirds of the way along appendage 1
(fig. 65H). Anal point not expanded distally, more pointed at tip
(fig. 65M). Hypopygium fig. 166B— **P. uncinatum** Goetghebuer

Genus PHAENOPSECTRA Kieffer

1   Abdomen dark brown to black. Hypopygium fig. 166C—
Phaenopsectra flavipes (Meigen)

—   Abdomen green. Hypopygium fig. 166D—
P. punctipes (Wiedemann)

The hypopygia of these two species are very similar but the coloration of the abdomen
appears to be a reliable character.

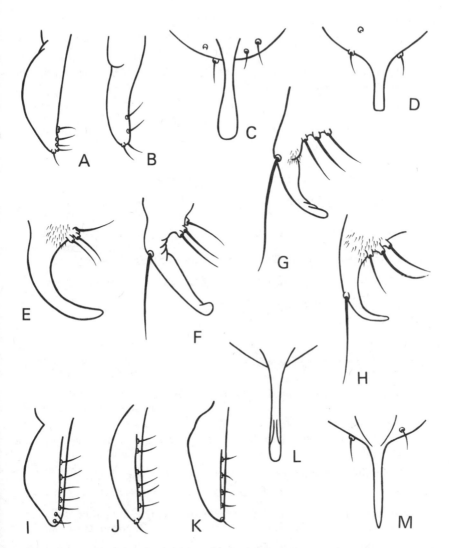

Fig. 65   A-B, gonostyli of: A, *Paratendipes albimanus*; B, *P. nudisquama*; C-D, anal points of: C, *P. albimanus*; D, *P. nudisquama*; E-H, appendages I of: E, *Pentapedilum nubens*; F, *P. sordens*; G, *P. tritum*; H, *P. uncinatum*; I-K, gonostyli of: I, *P. sordens*; J, *P. tritum*; K, *P. uncinatum*; L-M, anal points of: L, *P. tritum*; M, *P. uncinatum*.

Genus POLYPEDILUM Kieffer

1 Anal tergite with a lobe on each side of the anal point (fig. 66A-E). Appendage 1 broad, pad-like (fig. 66G)— **2**

— Anal tergite without such lobes (fig. 67A-B). Appendage 1 in the form of a hook (fig. 66F, H)— **6**

2 Anal point slender (fig. 66A). Hypopygium fig. 167A—
Polypedilum apfelbecki (Strobl)

— Anal point rather broad (fig. 66B-E)— **3**

3 Wing membrane with distinct dark markings— **4**

— Wing membrane unmarked— **5**

4 Anal point broadest subapically (fig. 66B). Hypopygium fig. 167B— **P. bicrenatum** Kieffer
(*Chironomus (Polypedilum) flavonervosus* Staeg., Edwards 1929)

— Anal point broadest medially (fig. 66C). Hypopygium fig. 167C— **P. pullum** (Zetterstedt)
(*Chironomus (Polypedilum) prolixitarsis* Lundst. 1916, Edwards 1929)

5(3) Lateral lobes of anal tergite rather broad (fig. 66D). Hypopygium fig. 167D— **P. quadriguttatum** Kieffer

— Lateral lobes more slender (fig. 66E). Hypopygium fig. 168A— **P. scalaenum** (Schrank)

6(1) Appendage 1 with a posterior lobe bearing at least one long seta (fig. 66F,H)— **7**

— Appendage 1 not as above, slender and curved (fig. 67D,F)— **8**

7 Posterior lobe of appendage 1 bearing a single long seta (fig. 66F). Hypopygium fig. 168B— **P. convictum** (Walker)

— Posterior lobe of appendage 1 bearing 4 or 5 long setae (fig. 66H). Hypopygium fig. 168C— **P. cultellatum** Goetghebuer

8(6) Wings distinctly marked (fig. 66I). Hypopygium fig. 168D— **P. laetum** (Meigen)

— Wings unmarked or at most with very faint markings— **9**

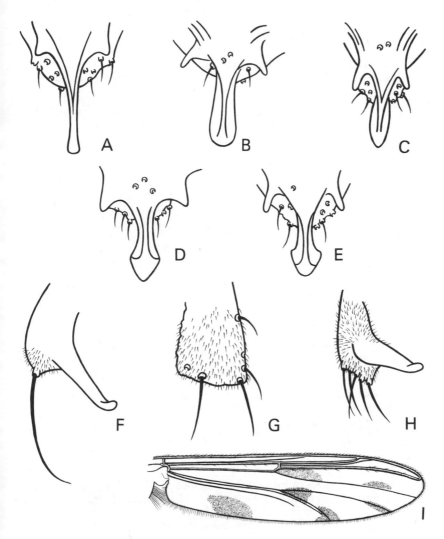

Fig. 66 A-E, anal tergites of: A, *Polypedilum apfelbecki*; B, *P. bicrenatum*; C, *P. pullum*; D, *P. quadriguttatum*; E, *P. scalaenum*; F-H, appendages 1 of: F, *P. convictum*; G, *P. apfelbecki*; H, *P. cultellatum*; I, wing of *P. laetum*.

9 Abdomen pale, sometimes darkened distally—   10

— Abdomen uniformly dark brown-black—   11

10 Anal point parallel-sided, rounded distally.   Anal tergite rounded
    (fig. 67A).   Hypopygium fig. 169A— **Polypedilum acutum** Kieffer

— Anal point tapered, longer and more slender.   Anal tergite triangular
    (fig. 67B).   Hypopygium fig. 169B—   **P. pedestre** (Meigen)
    (Chironomus (Microtendipes) fuscipennis Mg., Edwards 1929)

11(9) Antennal ratio 2·0 or more—   12

— Antennal ratio not exceeding 1·7—   13

12 Halteres white with darkened knob.   Anterior tarsus with a short
    beard.   Hypopygium fig. 169C—   **P. nubeculosum** (Meigen)

— Halteres entirely pale.   Tarsus not bearded.   Hypopygium as in *P.
    nubeculosum*—   **P. leucopum** (Meigen)

Although Coe (1950) recorded this species from Yorkshire, no British specimens were
found in the British Museum (Natural History) collection.   It may be only a variety of *P.
nubeculosum*.

13(11) Gonostylus short and broad (fig. 67C).   Appendage 1 slender,
    curved, lateral seta arising in proximal half (fig. 67D).   Hypopygium
    fig. 169D—   **P. arundinetum** Goetghebuer

— Gonostylus long and more slender (fig. 67E).   Appendage 1 robust
    and almost straight, lateral seta arising in distal half (fig. 67F).
    Hypopygium fig. 170A—   **P. albicorne** (Meigen)

Genus PSEUDOCHIRONOMUS Malloch

Only one species is known from Britain.   The conspicuous spur on
the anterior tibia (fig. 49G) and the characteristic hypopygium (fig.
170B) are sufficient to distinguish it—
                        Pseudochironomus prasinatus (Staeger)

Genus SERGENTIA Kieffer

The single species recorded from the British Isles may be identified
from the characters mentioned in the key to genera.   Hypopygium
fig. 170C—   **Sergentia coracina** (Zetterstedt)

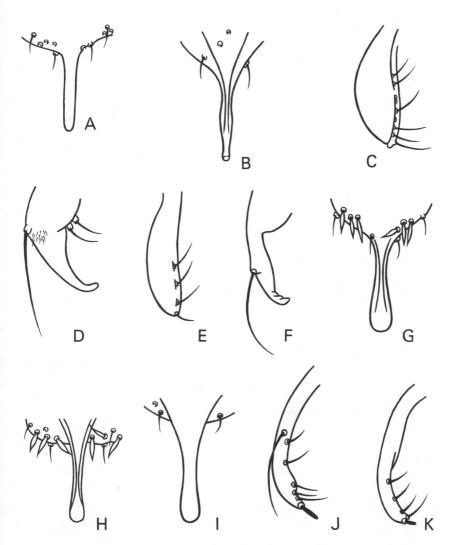

Fig. 67 A-B, anal points of: A, *Polypedilum acutum*; B, *P. pedestre*; C-D, *Polypedilum arundinetum*; C, gonostylus; D, appendage 1; E-F, *P. albicorne*: E, gonostylus; F, appendage 1; G-I, anal points of: G, *Stenochironomus fascipennis*; H, *S. gibbus*; I, *S. hibernicus*; J-K, appendages 2 of: J, *S. gibbus*; K, *S. hibernicus*.

Genus STENOCHIRONOMUS Kieffer

1   Anal point slender, scarcely expanded distally (fig. 67H).   Appendage
    2 with a long lateral seta (fig. 67J).   Hypopygium fig. 171A—
                          Stenochironomus gibbus (Fabricius)

—   Anal point broader, clubbed distally (fig. 67G, I).   Appendage 2
    without a long lateral seta (fig. 67K)—   **2**

2   Gonostylus tapered for some distance subapically.   Anal tergite
    bearing broad lamellar setae flanking the anal point (fig. 67G).
    Hypopygium fig. 170D—   **S. fascipennis** (Zetterstedt)

—   Gonostylus parallel-sided and broadly rounded distally.   Anal tergite
    with simple setae only (fig. 67I).   Hypopygium fig. 171B—
                             S. hibernicus (Edwards)

Genus STICTOCHIRONOMUS Kieffer

1   Wing membrane with several dark spots—   **2**

—   A single dark spot is present around r-m or else r-m and adjacent
    veins black, otherwise wing unmarked—   **3**

2   Gonostylus slender, with a few weak setae distally (fig. 68A).
    Appendage 1 hooked apically, otherwise almost straight (fig.
    68B).   Wing markings rather faint.   Hypopygium fig. 171C—
                        Stictochironomus pictulus (Meigen)

—   Gonostylus more robust, with a number of strong setae distally (fig.
    68C).   Apical half of appendage 1 strongly curved (fig.
    68D).   Wing markings distinct.   Hypopygium fig. 171D—
                            S. maculipennis (Meigen)

3(1) Appendage 1 almost straight (fig. 68E).   Cross-vein r-m and
    neighbouring veins black, membrane unmarked.   Hypopygium fig.
    172A—   **S. rosenschoeldi** (Zetterstedt)

—   Apical section of appendage 1 strongly curved (fig. 68F).   Wing
    membrane with a small dark spot around r-m.   Hypopygium fig.
    172B—   **S. sticticus** (Fabricius)
    (Chironomus (Stictochironomus) histrio Fab., Edwards 1929)

Genus XENOCHIRONOMUS Kieffer

The only species belonging to this genus may be easily identified from
its characteristic hypopygium (fig. 172C)—
                        Xenochironomus xenolabis (Kieffer)

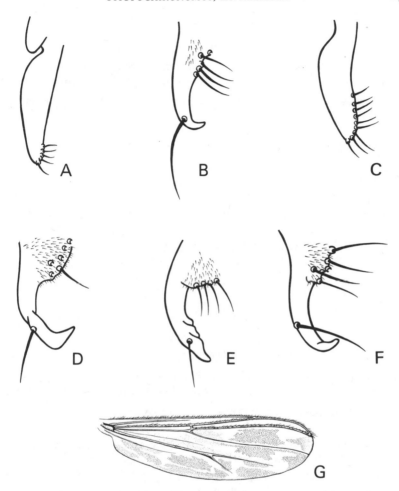

Fig. 68 A-B, *Stictochironomus pictulus*: A, gonostylus; B, appendage 1; C-D, *S. maculipennis*: C, gonostylus; D, appendage 1; E-F, appendages 1 of: E, *S. rosenschoeldi*; F, *S. sticticus*; G, wing of *Zavreliella marmorata*.

Genus ZAVRELIELLA Kieffer

The male of the only species ascribed to this genus is unknown. According to Edwards (1929) the species is sometimes, perhaps always, parthenogenetic. The female is easily identified by the numerous dark grey spots on the wings (fig. 68G)—

Zavreliella marmorata (van der Wulp)

Tribe TANYTARSINI

Genus CLADOTANYTARSUS Kieffer

1   Thorax entirely dark brown/black, abdomen dark brown. Hypopygium fig. 173A—   **Cladotanytarsus atridorsum** Kieffer

—   Ground colour of thorax greenish with scutal stripes reddish or blackish. Abdomen green—   **2**

2   Antennal ratio 0·7-1·0. Small species, wing length *c.* 1·5 mm. Hypopygium fig. 173B—   **C. vanderwulpi** (Edwards)

—   Antennal ratio >1·1. Larger species, wing length 2-2·5 mm.—   **3**

3   Scutal stripes light brown or reddish. Hypopygium fig. 173C—   **C. mancus** (Walker)

—   Scutal stripes black. Hypopygium fig. 173D—   **C. nigrovittatus** Goetghebuer

Genus MICROPSECTRA Kieffer
(Reiss 1969)
(Säwedal 1976)

1   Combs of posterior tibia contiguous each with a short spur. Hypopygium fig. 174A—   **Micropsectra tenellula** (Goetghebuer)

—   Combs of posterior tibia fused, without spurs—   **2**

2   Very small (wing length <2·1 mm) pale green species, scutal stripes scarcely differentiated. Hypopygium fig. 174B—   **M. attenuata** Reiss

—   Larger species (wing length >2·5 mm). Scutal stripes distinct—   **3**

3   Anal point narrow, triangular (fig. 69A)—   **4**

—   Anal point broad, parallel-sided and rounded distally (fig. 69B)—   **8**

4   Appendage 2a with a clump of broad, leaf-like setae (fig. 69C). Hypopygium fig. 174C—   **M. lindrothi** Goetghebuer (*M. foliata* Laville 1965)

—   Appendage 2a with spoon-shaped setae (fig. 69D)—   **5**

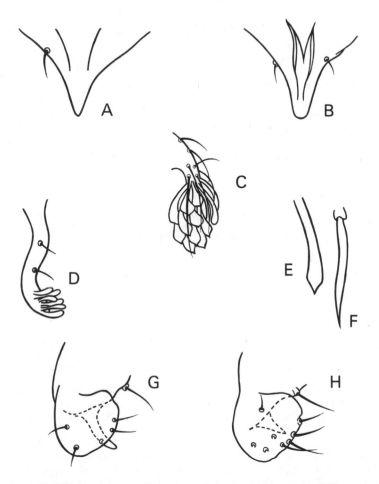

Fig. 69 A-B, anal points of: A, *Micropsectra lindrothi*; B, *M. aristata*; C-D, appendages 2a of: C, *M. lindrothi*; D, *M. recurvata*; E-F, lamellar setae of appendages 2a of: E, *M. aristata*; F, *M. fusca*; G-H, appendages 1 and 1a of: G, *M. bidentata*; H, *M. atrofasciata*.

5 Appendage 2a strongly curved (fig. 69D). Hypopygium fig. 174D—
M. recurvata (Goetghebuer)

— Appendage 2a more or less straight—   6

6   Abdomen mainly green, apical segments usually brown.   Antennal
    ratio 1·0-1·3.   Hypopygium fig. 175A—
                            Micropsectra junci (Meigen)
    (Tanytarsus (Micropsectra) subviridis Goet., Edwards 1929)

—   Entirely dark brown.   Antennal ratio >1·3—   7

7   Appendage 2a short (47-62 µm), not reaching tip of appendage 1.
    Hypopygium fig. 175B—   **M. notescens** (Walker)
    (Tanytarsus (Micropsectra) brunnipes (Zett.), Edwards 1929)
    (Micropsectra praecox (Meigen 1818), Kloet & Hincks 1975)

—   Appendage 2a longer (74-89 µm) reaching approximately to tip of
    appendage 2.   Hypopygium fig. 175C—   **M. apposita** (Walker)

The male is not distinguishable from the male of *M. contracta* Reiss, although the female
and pupa are distinct. (Säwedal 1976).   *M. apposita* occurs in flowing water (springs and
streams) whereas *M. contracta* is typical of the deeper parts of lakes (below *c.* 5 m).

8(3) Setae of appendage 2 spoon-shaped (fig. 69D)—   9

—   Setae of appendage 2 broad, strap-like (fig. 69E-F)—   10

9   Appendage 1a long, extending beyond appendage 1 (fig. 69G).
    Abdomen green.   Hypopygium fig. 175D—
                            M. bidentata (Goetghebuer)
    (Tanytarsus (Micropsectra) retusus Goet., Edwards 1929)

—   Appendage 1a shorter, not reaching margin of appendage 1 (fig. 69H).
    Abdomen green, the tergites often with narrow brown bands.
    Hypopygium fig. 176A—   **M. atrofasciata** Kieffer

10(8) Lamellar setae of appendage 2a uniformly tapered towards the fine
    apex (fig. 69F), reaching almost to tip of appendage 2.
    Hypopygium fig. 176B—   **M. fusca** (Meigen)

—   Lamellar setae of appendage 2a abruptly tapered distally, ending in a
    fine point (fig. 69E), extending about half way along appendage 2.
    Hypopygium fig. 176C—   **M. aristata** Pinder

Genus PARAPSECTRA Reiss
(Reiss 1969)

1   Gonostylus and gonocoxite about equal in length.   Hypopygium fig.
      177A—   **Parapsectra chionophila** (Edwards)

—   Gonostylus about twice as long as gonocoxite.   Hypopygium fig.
      177B—   **P. nana** (Meigen)
      (Tanytarsus (Micropsectra) monticola Edwards)

Genus PARATANYTARSUS Bause
(Reiss 1968)

1 Appendage 2a with a distal clump of lamellar setae (e.g. fig. 70B)— **2**

— Appendage 2a with simple setae only (e.g. fig. 71A)—   **7**

2 Median setae of anal tergite arising from elongate bases (fig. 70A). Hypopygium fig. 177C— **Paratanytarsus bituberculatus** Edwards

— Median setae not arising from elongate bases—   **3**

3 Appendage 1a deeply divided into two lobes (fig. 70C).   Hypopygium fig. 178A—   **P. intricatus** (Goetghebuer)

— Appendage 1a not as above—   **4**

4 Appendage 2a with long lanceolate setae extending beyond appendage 2 (fig. 70D).   Hypopygium fig. 178B—
P. penicillatus (Goetghebuer)

— Setae of appendage 2a much shorter, not reaching beyond appendage 2—   **5**

5 Inner margin of appendage 2 expanded in distal half (fig. 70F). Lamellar setae of appendage 2a club-shaped (fig. 70E). Hypopygium fig. 178C—   **P. laetipes** (Zetterstedt)

— Appendage 2 not as above.   Lamellar setae of 2a tapered distally (fig. 70, G-H)—   **6**

6 Inner margin of gonostylus with a distinct bulge subapically (fig. 70I).   Appendage 1 almost rectangular (fig. 70K).   Hypopygium fig. 178D—   **P. laccophilus** (Edwards)

— Inner margin of gonostylus more or less straight (fig. 70J). Appendage 1 roughly triangular (fig. 70L). Hypopygium fig. 179A—   **P. tenuis** (Meigen)

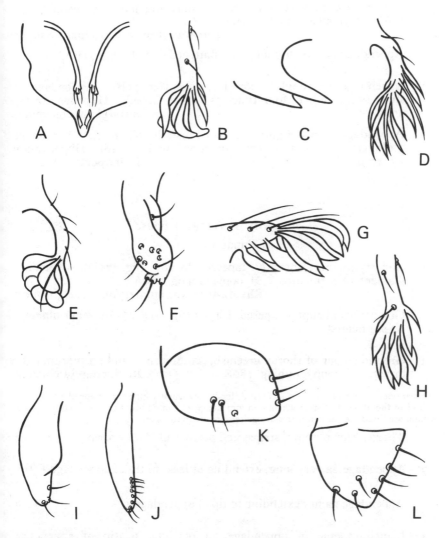

Fig. 70 A, anal tergite of *Paratanytarsus bituberculatus*; B-C, *P. intricatus*: B, appendage 2a; C, appendage 1a; D-E, appendages 2a of: D, *P. penicillatus*: E, *P. laetipes*; F, appendage 2 of *P. laetipes*; G-H, appendages 2a of: G, *P. laccophilus*; H, *P. tenuis*; I-J, gonostyli of: I, *P. laccophilus*; J, *P. tenuis*; K-L, appendages 1 of: K, *P. laccophilus*; L, *P. tenuis*.

7(1) Appendage 2a very long (90-120 μm) and flattened distally (fig. 71A). Hypopygium fig. 179B—
Paratanytarsus austriacus Kieffer

— Appendage 2a <60 μm long, not flattened distally (fig. 71B-C)— **8**

8 Appendage 2 strongly clubbed apically (fig. 71B). Appendage 2a short (<40 μm), c. four times as long as broad. Hypopygium fig. 179C— **P. natvigi** (Goetghebuer)

— Appendage 2 only slightly expanded distally (fig. 71C). Appendage 2a longer (c. 50 μm), c. seven times as long as broad. Hypopygium fig. 179D— **P. inopertus** (Walker)

Genus RHEOTANYTARSUS Bause

(Lehmann 1970)

1 Gonostylus not abruptly tapered distally (fig. 71D). Antennal filament 12-segmented. Hypopygium fig. 180A—
Rheotanytarsus curtistylus (Goetghebuer)

— Gonostylus abruptly tapered distally (fig. 71E). Antennal filament 13-segmented— **2**

2 Ground colour of thorax greenish, scutal stripes and postnotum light brown. Hypopygium fig. 180B— **R. cf. ringei** Lehmann

This species is very similar to *ringei* but differs in the slightly different shape of appendage 1 and in the absence of microtrichia on appendage 1. In addition the anal tergite bands which are fused medially in *ringei* are quite separate in this species.

— Thorax brown, scutal stripes and postnotum dark brown— **3**

3 Appendage 2a very long, extending at least to tip of appendage 1 (fig. 71F-G)— **4**

— Appendage 2a not extending to tip of appendage 1— **5**

4 Lamellar setae of appendage 2a reaching to tip of appendage 2. Posterior margin of appendage 1 produced into a distinct 'beak' (fig. 71H). Hypopygium fig. 180C— **R. photophilus** Goetghebuer

— Lamellar setae of appendage 2a ending well before tip of appendage 2. Posterior margin of appendage 1 not or scarcely produced (fig. 71I). Hypopygium fig. 180D— **R. pentapoda** Kieffer

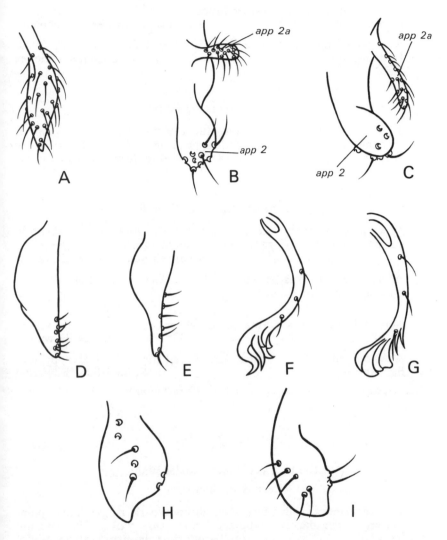

Fig. 71   A, appendage 2a of *Paratanytarsus austriacus*; B-C, appendages 2 and 2a of: B, *P. natvigi*; C, *P. inopertus*; D-E, gonostyli of: D, *Rheotanytarsus curtistylus*; E, *R. photophilus*; F-G, appendages 2a of: F, *R. photophilus*; G, *R. pentapoda*; H-I, appendages 1 of: H, *R. photophilus*; I, *R. pentapoda*.

5(3) Anal point (fig. 72A) rather broad.   Appendage 1 as in fig. 72C.
Hypopygium fig. 181A—   **Rheotanytarsus reissi** Lehmann

— Anal point (fig. 72B) more slender.   Appendage 1 as in fig. 72D.
Hypopygium fig. 181B—   **R. muscicola** Kieffer

Genus STEMPELLINA Bause

There is only one British representative of this genus.   The shape of
the anal point (fig. 72E) and appendage 1 (fig. 72F) are very
distinctive.   Hypopygium fig. 181C— **Stempellina bausei** (Kieffer)

Genus STEMPELLINELLA Brundin

1   Appendage 2a very slender (fig. 72G).   Anal point abruptly
narrowed apically (fig. 72J).   Hypopygium fig. 181D—
Stempellinella minor (Edwards)

— Appendage 2a broader (fig. 72H-I).   Anal point not abruptly
narrowed apically—   **2**

2   Antennal ratio c. 0·5.   Anal point slender (fig. 72K).   Hypopygium
fig. 182A—   **S. brevis** (Edwards)

— Antennal ratio c. 1·5.   Anal point broad (fig. 72L).   Hypopygium
fig. 182B—   **S. flavidula** (Edwards)

A fourth species *S. cuneipennis* (Edwards) is known from the female only (Edwards 1929).

Genus TANYTARSUS van der Wulp
(Reiss & Fittkau 1971)

1   Tips of femora and tibiae with distinct dark rings.   Anal point
bearing three darkly chitinized combs (fig. 73A).   Hypopygium
fig. 182C—   **Tanytarsus signatus** (van der Wulp)

— Legs not ringed.   Combs on anal point not as above or absent—   **2**

2   Anal point bearing a pair of long processes (fig. 73B)—   **3**

— Anal point lacking such structures—   **4**

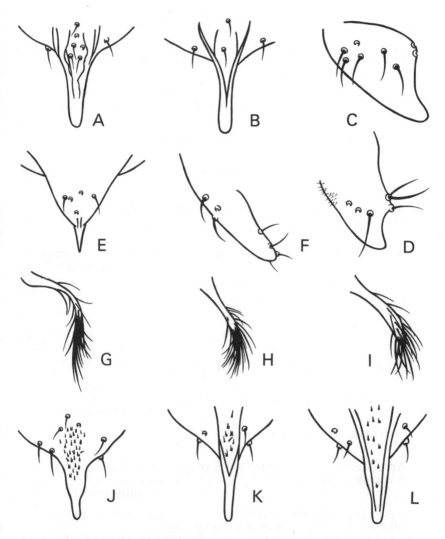

Fig. 72   A-B, anal points of: A, *Rheotanytarsus reissi*; B, *R. muscicola*; C-D, appendages
1 of: C, *R. reissi*; D, *R. muscicola*; E-F, *Stempellina bausei*: E, anal point; F,
appendage 1; G-I, appendages 2a of: G, *Stempellinella minor*; H, *S. brevis*; I, *S.
flavidula*; J-L, anal points of: J. *S. minor*; K, *S. brevis*; L, *S. flavidula*.

3   Dark brown species.   Hypopygium fig. 182D—
    (*T. reflexens* Edwards 1929)   **Tanytarsus triangularis** Goetghebuer

—   Pale green, sometimes with light brown scutal stripes.   Hypopygium
    fig. 183A—   **T. arduennensis** Goetghebuer
    (*T. richmondensis* Edwards 1929)

4(2) Dorsal surface of anal point bearing several clusters of short dark
    spines (e.g. fig. 73C)—   **5**

—   Anal point without such groups of spines—   **22**

5   Anal tergite bands fused posteriorly to form a Y-shape (e.g. fig.
    73D)—   **6**

—   Anal tergite bands well separated but occasionally linked by a broad
    darkened median zone—   **10**

6   Anal point with a sub-apical field of unusually long dark spines (fig.
    73D).   Hypopygium fig. 183B—   **T. usmaensis** Pagast
    (*T. junci* (Mg.) Goet., Edwards 1929)

—   Spines of anal point much shorter—   **7**

7   Appendages 2 and 2a strongly curved, the latter very long (fig.
    73E).   Hypopygium fig. 183C—   **T. sylvaticus** (van der Wulp)

—   Appendages 2 and 2a not strongly curved, 2a shorter—   **8**

8   Gonostylus spatulate (fig. 73F).   Hypopygium fig. 183D—
                                          T. miriforceps (Kieffer)

—   Gonostylus not spatulate—   **9**

9   Appendage 1a slender, strongly S-shaped, and appendage 1 roughly
    trapezoidal in outline (fig. 73G).   Hypopygium fig. 184A—
                                         T. pallidicornis (Walker)

—   Appendage 1a more robust and less strongly curved; appendage 1
    obovate (fig. 73H).   Hypopygium fig. 184B—
                                   T. buchonius Reiss & Fittkau

10(5) Appendage 1a reaching at least to margin of appendage 1 and
    usually well beyond—   **11**

—   Appendage 1a short, not reaching margin of appendage 1—   **19**

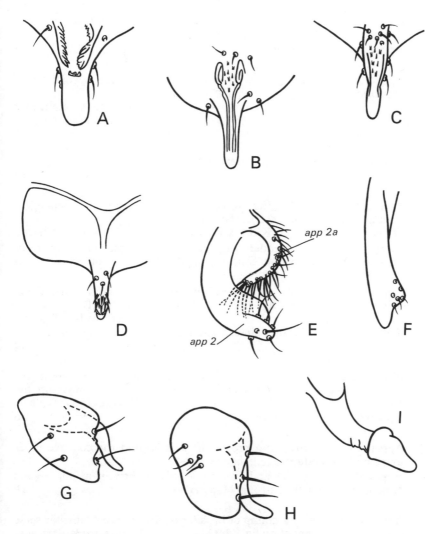

Fig. 73 A-D, anal points of: A, *Tanytarsus signatus*; B, *T. triangularis*; C, *T. pallidicornis*; D, *T. usmaensis*; E, appendages 2 and 2a of *T. sylvaticus*; F, gonostylus of *T. miriforceps*; G-H, appendages 1 and 1a of: G, *T. pallidicornis*; H, *T. buchonius*; I, appendage 1a of *T. brundini*.

11   Appendage 1a spirally twisted and distally flattened (fig. 73I). Hypopygium fig. 184C—   **Tanytarsus brundini** Lindeberg
     (*T. curticornis* Kieff., Edwards 1929)
—   Appendage 1a not as above—   **12**

12   Appendage 2a very long with distal setae extending beyond tip of appendage 2 (fig. 74A). Hypopygium fig. 184D—
                                                  T. lestagei Goetghebuer
Lindeberg (1967) divided *T. lestagei* into nine sister species on ecological, phenological, behavioural and morphological grounds. They are, however, not separable as individuals.

—   Appendage 2a much shorter, setae ending well before tip of appendage 2—   **13**

13   Anal point very broad (fig. 74B).   Posterior margin of appendage 1 strongly concave (fig. 74C).   Hypopygium fig. 185A—
     (*T. norvegicus* Kieffer, Kloet & Hincks 1975)   **T. niger** Anderson
—   Anal point more slender (e.g. fig. 74D).   Posterior margin of appendage 1 not strongly concave, usually distinctly convex—   **14**

14   Appendage 1 roughly obovate in outline and bearing a ventro-distal field of small papillae (fig. 74E).   Hypopygium fig. 185B—
                                                 T. eminulus (Walker)
—   Appendage 1 differently shaped and lacking ventro-distal papillae—
                                                                     15

15   Appendage 1 with a constriction which tends to set apart the posterior region as a distinct knob (fig. 74F).   Hypopygium fig. 185C—   **T. ejuncidus** (Walker)
—   Appendage 1 not as above—   **16**

16   Appendage 1a broad and projecting well beyond the concave inner margin of appendage 1 (e.g. fig. 74G)—   **17**
—   Appendage 1a slender and projecting only slightly, if at all, beyond appendage 1, which is strongly tapered—   **18**

17   Appendage 2a with a clump of broad, distally rounded lamellar setae (fig. 74I).   Hypopygium fig. 185D—   **T. palettaris** Verneaux
     (*T. verruculosus* Goet., Edwards 1929)
—   Lamellar setae of appendage 2a more slender and terminating in several fine points (fig. 74J).   Hypopygium fig. 186A—
     (*T. arduennensis* Goet., Edwards 1929)   **T. heusdensis** Goetghebuer
In order to see the lamellar setae clearly it is necessary to dissect the hypopygium and to squash appendage 1a.

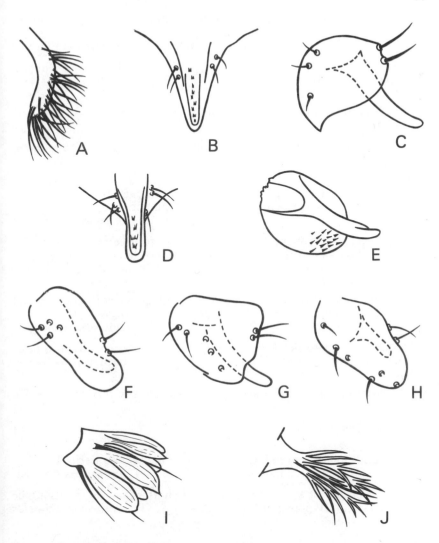

Fig. 74   A, appendage 2a of *Tanytarsus lestagei*; B-C, *T. niger*: B, anal point; C, appendages 1 and 1a; D-E, *T. eminulus*: D, anal point; E, appendages 1 and 1a (ventral); F-H, appendages 1 and 1a of: F, *T. ejuncidus*; G, *T. heusdensis*; H, *T. gracilentus*; I-J, appendages 2a of: I, *T. palettaris*; J, *T. heusdensis*.

18(16) Anal point rounded distally (fig. 75A). Appendage 2 clubbed distally (fig. 75B). Hypopygium fig. 186B—
Tanytarsus holochlorus Edwards

— Anal point distally truncate (fig. 75C). Appendage 2 not clubbed. Hypopygium fig. 186C— **T. fimbriatus** Reiss & Fittkau

19(10) Groups of spines on anal point arranged in a single row (fig. 75D)— **20**

— Groups of spines scattered over the dorsal surface of the anal point (e.g. fig. 75G-H)— **21**

20 Long axis of appendage 1 more or less parallel with the body axis (fig. 75E). Appendage 1a absent. Hypopygium fig. 186D—
T. gregarius Kieffer

— Appendage 1 oriented more or less transversely (fig. 75F). Appendage 1a present but very short. Hypopygium fig. 187A—
T. inaequalis Goetghebuer

21(19) Anal point broad (fig. 75G). Appendage 2a with a short, but distinct, basal lobe (fig. 75I). Hypopygium fig. 187B—
T. gracilentus Holmgren

— Anal point more slender (fig. 75H). Appendage 2a without a basal lobe. Hypopygium fig. 187C— **T. bathophilus** Kieffer

22(4) Inner margin of appendage 1 produced into two distinct lobes (fig. 75J-K)— **23**

— Appendage 1 not as above— **24**

23 Posterior lobe of appendage 1 at least as long as the anterior lobe (fig. 75J). Hypopygium fig. 187D— **T. excavatus** Edwards

— Posterior lobe of appendage 1 distinctly shorter than the anterior lobe (fig. 75K). Hypopygium fig. 188A— **T. nemorosus** Edwards

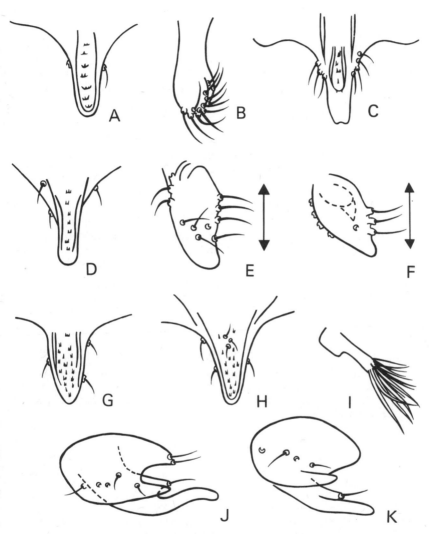

Fig. 75   A-B, *Tanytarsus holochlorus*: A, anal point; B, appendage 2; C-D, anal point of:
C, *T. fimbriatus*; D, *T. gregarius*; E-F, appendages 1 of: E, *T. gregarius*; F, *T.
inaequalis* (arrows indicate the direction of the main body axis); G-H, anal
points of: G, *T. gracilentus*; H, *T. bathophilus*; I, appendage 2a of *T.
gracilentus*; J-K, appendages 1 and 1a of: J, *T. excavatus*; K, *T. nemorosus*.

24(22) Anal tergite bearing a cluster of 2-6 unusually long, dark setae (fig. 76A)—   **25**

— Anal tergite without such a cluster of setae—   **26**

25   Appendage 1 strongly concave posteriorly (fig. 76E).   Hypopygium fig. 188B—   **Tanytarsus verralli** Goetghebuer

— Posterior margin of appendage 1 convex (fig. 76D).   Hypopygium fig. 188C—   **T. debilis** (Meigen)

26(24) Lateral teeth of anal tergite unusually large, bifurcate and conspicuously darkened (fig. 76C).   Hypopygium fig. 188D—
      T. quadridentatus Brundin

— Anal tergite lacking lateral teeth—   **27**

27   Appendage 1 strongly concave medially, 1a somewhat expanded distally (fig. 76F).   Hypopygium fig. 189A—
      T. lactescens Edwards

— Inner margin of appendage 1 straight or only weakly concave, 1a not expanded distally (fig. 76G).   Hypopygium fig. 189B—
      T. glabrescens Edwards

Genus ZAVRELIA Kieffer

The only British representative of the genus is easily recognized from its distinctive hypopygium (fig. 189C).   The anal point (fig. 76H) is particularly characteristic—   **Zavrelia pentatoma** Kieffer
(*Tanytarsus (Z.) nigritulus* Goet., Edwards 1929)

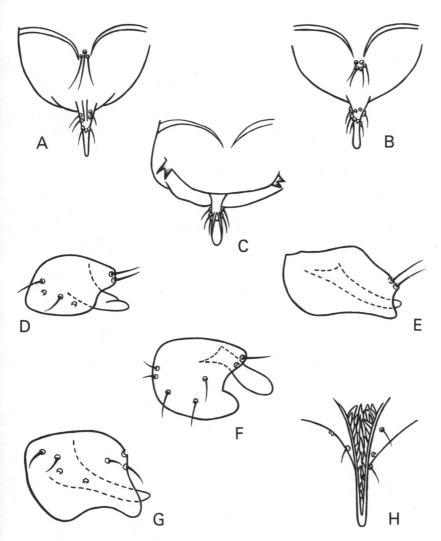

Fig. 76 A-C, anal tergites of: A, *Tanytarsus verralli*; B, *T. debilis*; C, *T. quadridentatus*;
D-G, appendages 1 and 1a of: D, *T. debilis*; E, *T. verralli*; F, *T. lactescens*; G, *T. glabrescens*; H, anal point of *Zavrelia pentatoma*.

ACKNOWLEDGMENTS

This work would never have reached fruition without the generosity of Dr E. J. Fittkau and Dr F. Reiss of the Max-Planck Institut für Limnologie in Plön (now at the Zoologische Sammlung des Bayerischen Staates), and the Trustees of the British Museum in lending many specimens from their respective collections.

Help and advice has been freely forthcoming from many individuals and I would particularly like to thank the following: Dr K. Aagaard, Mr P. S. Cranston, Dr H. Disney, Dr E. J. Fittkau, Mr A. M. Hutson, Dr M. Learner, Dr P. S. Maitland, Dr F. Reiss and Dr L. Säwedal.   Most of all my thanks are due to Mrs A. M. Matthews for the long hours she has spent peering down microscopes, executing the illustrations without which this key would have been inestimably the poorer.

A significant proportion of the financial support for this work was provided by the Department of the Environment (Contract No. DGR 480/33).

REFERENCES

Brundin, L. (1956). Zur Systematik der Orthocladiinae. *Rep. Inst. Freshwat. Res. Drottningholm,* **37,** 1-185.

Coe, R. L. (1950). Family Chironomidae. *Handbk Ident. Br. Insects,* **9,** 2, 121-206.

Disney, R. H. L. (1975). A key to the larvae, pupae and adults of the British Dixidae (Diptera). *Scient. Publs Freshwat. Biol. Ass.* No. 31, 78 pp.

Downes, J. A. & Colless, D. H. (1967). Mouthparts of the biting and bloodsucking type in Tanyderidae and Chironomidae. *Nature, Lond.* **214,** 1355-6.

Edwards, F. W. (1929). British non-biting midges (Diptera, Chironomidae). *Trans. R. ent. Soc. Lond.* **77,** 279-429.

Fittkau, E. J. (1962). Die Tanypodinae (Diptera, Chironomidae). Die Tribus Anatopyniini, Macropelopiini und Pentaneurini. *Abh. Larvalsyst. Insekten,* **6,** 1-453.

Fittkau, E. J. & Lehmann, J. (1970). Revision der Gattung *Microcricotopus* Thien. u. Harn. (Dipt. Chironomidae). *Int. Revue ges. Hydrobiol. Hydrogr.* **55,** 391-402.

Hirvenoja, M. (1973). Revision der Gattung *Cricotopus* van der Wulp und ihrer Verwandten (Diptera, Chironomidae). *Annls zool. Fenn.* **10,** 1-363.

Keyl, H.-G. & Keyl, I. (1959). Die cytologische Artdifferenzierung der Chironomiden. 1. Bestimmungstabelle für die Gattung *Chironomus* auf Grund der Speicheldrüsen-Chromosomen. *Arch. Hydrobiol.* **56,** 43-57.

Kloet, G. S. & Hincks, W. D. (1975). A check list of British insects. (2nd edition). Part 5: Diptera and Siphonaptera. *Handbk Ident. Br. Insects,* **11,** 139 pp.

Lehmann, J. (1969). Die europäischen Arten der Gattung *Rheocricotopus* Thien. und Harn. und drei neue Artvertreter dieser Gattung aus der Orientalis (Diptera, Chironomidae). *Arch. Hydrobiol.* **66,** 348-81.

Lehmann, J. (1970a). Revision der europäischen Arten (Imagines ♂♂) der Gattung *Parachironomus* Lenz (Diptera, Chironomidae). *Hydrobiologia,* **33,** 129-58.

Lehmann, J. (1970b). Revision der europäischen Arten (Imagines ♂♂ und Puppen ♂♂) der Gattung *Rheotanytarsus* Bause (Diptera, Chironomidae). *Zool. Anz.* **185,** 344-78.

Lehmann, J. (1972). Revision der europäischen Arten (Puppen ♂♂ und Imagines ♂♂) der Gattung *Eukiefferiella* Thienemann. *Beitr. Ent.* **22,** 347-405.

Lindeberg, B. (1967). Sibling species delimitation in the *Tanytarsus lestagei* aggregate (Diptera, Chironomidae). *Annls zool. fenn.* **4,** 45-86.

Pagast, F. (1947). Systematik und Verbreitung der um die Gattung *Diamesa* gruppierten Chironomiden. *Arch. Hydrobiol.* **41**, 435-596.

Reiss, F. (1968). Ökologische und systematische Untersuchungen an Chironomiden (Diptera) des Bodensees. *Arch. Hydrobiol.* **64**, 176-323.

Reiss, F. (1969a). Revision der Gattung *Micropsectra* Kieff., 1909. 1. Die *attenuata*-Gruppe der Gattung *Micropsectra*. Beschreibung 5 neuer Arten aus Mitteleuropa und Nordafrika. *Dt. ent. Z.* **16**, 431-49.

Reiss, F. (1969b). Die neue europäisch verbreitete Chironomidengattung *Parapsectra* mit einem brachypteren Artvertreter aus Mooren (Diptera). *Arch. Hydrobiol.* **66**, 192-211.

Reiss, F. & Fittkau, E. J. (1971). Taxonomie und Ökologie europäisch verbreiteter *Tanytarsus*-Arten (Chironomidae Diptera). *Arch. Hydrobiol.* *(Suppl.)* **40**, 75-200.

Saether, O. A. (1971). Notes on general morphology and terminology of the Chironomidae (Diptera). *Can. Ent.* **103**, 1237-60.

Saether, O. A. (1976). Revision of *Hydrobaenus, Trissocladius, Zalutschia, Paratrissocladius,* and some related genera (Diptera: Chironomidae). *Bull. Fish. Res. Bd Can.* **195**, 287 pp.

Saether, O. A. (1977). Taxonomic studies on Chironomidae: *Nanocladius, Pseudochironomus,* and the *Harnischia* complex. *Bull. Fish. Res. Bd Can.* **196**, 143 pp.

Säwedal, L. (1976). Revision of the *notescens*-group of the genus *Micropsectra* Kieffer, 1909 (Diptera, Chironomidae). *Entomologica scand.* **7**, 109-44.

Schlee, D. (1966). Präparation und Ermittlung von Messwerten an Chironomiden (Diptera). *Gewäss. Abwäss.* **41/42**, 169-93.

Schlee, D. (1968). Vergleichende Merkmalsanalyse zur Morphologie und Phylogenie der *Corynoneura*-Gruppe (Diptera, Chironomidae). *Stuttg. Beitr. Naturk.* **180**, 1-150.

Serra-Tosio, B. (1967). Taxonomie et écologie de *Diamesa* du groupe *latitarsis* (Diptera, Chironomidae). *Trav. Lab. Hydrobiol. Piscic. Univ. Grenoble,* **57-58**, 65-91.

Serra-Tosio, B. (1968). Taxonomie phylogénétique des Diamesini; les genres *Potthastia* Kieffer, *Sympotthastia* Pagast, *Parapotthastia* n.g. et *Lappodiamesa* n.g. (Diptera: Chironomidae). *Trav. Lab. Hydrobiol. Piscic. Univ. Grenoble,* **59-60**, 117-64.

Steedman, A. F. (1958). Dimethyl hydantoin formaldehyde: a new water-soluble resin for use as a mounting medium. *Q. Jl microsc. Sci.* **99**, 451-452.

Strenzke, K. (1959). Revision der Gattung *Chironomus* Meig. 1. Die Imagines von 15 norddeutschen Arten und Unterarten. *Arch. Hydrobiol.* **56**, 1-42.

Wülker, W. (1956). Zur Kenntnis der Gattung *Psectrocladius* Kieff. (Dipt. Chironom.). *Arch. Hydrobiol. (Suppl.)* **24**, 1-66.

INDEX TO GENERA AND SPECIES

Figures in **bold-face** type refer to the illustrations of hypopygia in Volume 2. Synonyms are given in parentheses.

SCIENTIFIC PUBLICATIONS

* Out of print.

Scientific Publication No. 37
Price to non-members £4·50
1978

TITUS WILSON & SON LTD.
KENDAL 2000/7/78
SBN 900386 32 0
ISSN 0367-1887